By Steven Blanshan

Copyright © 2015 Steven Blanshan

All rights reserved.

ISBN: 0692473130
ISBN-13: 978-0692473139

Library of Congress Control Number: 2015912338
Blanshan, Daphne Alabama

First printing, October 2015

This is a work of fiction. Names, characters, places, and incidents are either the product of the author's imagination or are used fictitiously, and any resemblance to actual persons, living or dead, business establishments, events, or locales is entirely coincidental.

awormnamedhank.com

For M-

CONTENTS

INTRODUCTION

Hello. I'm Hank. Contrary to the title of this amazing story I am not, repeat loudly, *not* a worm. That's just what my older brother calls me. As far as I know that is all he has ever called me. I imagine the day of my arrival into this world he said, "Hi, Worm." And then asked our mom if he could feed me dirt.

I have, involuntarily, eaten dirt 37 times. My older brother has hidden dirt in my cereal, my birthday cake, my mashed potatoes, my tomato soup, and on and on. I have become a dirt connoisseur. Every time I bite into my food I wait for his hideous laugh. No laugh, no dirt, safe to continue. If there's laughter, I'm eating dirt, and he quickly follows with a *hideous* laugh and, "Hey Worm, how's your dirt taste?"

I have two Super Friends named Isaac and Sue. We stopped calling each other best friends because Super is way cooler. Isaac lives two doors down in a big blue house, while Sue lives across the street. They are referred to as "only children" meaning they have no older brothers. As a result they have only eaten dirt once. It would be zero times, but after my birthday cake dirt surprise, Isaac and Sue took me to the backyard and grabbed up two big handfuls of dirt and ate it. They said no one should ever have to eat dirt on their birthday alone. They truly are Super Friends. Everyone wants to have a friend who will eat dirt with him; I have two.

I don't remember the first time I met Isaac or Sue. It's kind of like they were always there. Like a mosquito. You never really see a mosquito land on you.

You just look down and suddenly there it is. Not that I would ever compare Isaac or Sue to a bloodsucking parasite; that sounds more like my older brother Todd. He's sneaky like a mosquito.

Four months ago I was taking a bath. I even locked the bathroom door to ensure my privacy. One time my mom accidently came into the bathroom while I was changing and the embarrassment of my mom seeing me naked still haunts my dreams. So now tub time means lock the door.

Somehow Todd still got in, and he threw a handful of worms in the water. He laughed his hideous laugh and shouted, "Your real family missed you, Worm. Make sure to clean behind their ears." Followed by more laughter. Which was dumb. Worms don't have ears. I've learned a lot about worms. For instance, not only do worms not have ears they also don't have eyes. I would never tell Todd, but I actually kind of . . . sort of . . . like

worms. But please don't get confused by that. I AM NOT

A WORM!

THE MISSING OCTOPUS

Sue has this somewhat weird, somewhat cool thing her dad got her. It's an octopus. Not a living octopus, but a stuffed animal octopus. I didn't know about it for years. I guess she felt like she was too old for a favorite stuffed animal and was ashamed to tell Isaac and me about it. In fact, if it hadn't gone missing I'm not sure she would have ever told us.

This is how it all happened. One day we were all riding our bikes around the neighborhood. It was the beginning of summer, which is by far the best part of summer. Now don't get me wrong; all of summer is amazing, but there is something special about those first few weeks of freedom. The air is crisper, the sun shines just a little more brightly, the grass rises up just a little higher to meet your feet and help carry you along to the freedom that comes with day after day of no school. The middle of summer is a time that flows fast like quarters at an arcade, and before you know it you are left with no more time and you have no clue what happened to all those summer days. Then there is the end of summer where you wake up in the middle of the night in a cold sweat, the knowledge that school is hiding right around the corner.

There are a few times where a kid falls into the trap of thinking he can't wait to go BACK to school. These things can happen, usually to the younger generations of children who haven't yet learned the horrors of school, but in rare times it happens to all age children. Late one summer Isaac once said that he was actually looking forward to school starting. As soon as he said it out loud he grabbed his hands and threw them over his mouth. Look, a kid is allowed to like school, but he is never supposed to admit it and he is NEVER EVER supposed to miss it.

This day was the perfect start to summer. There were no clouds anywhere, Todd was hanging out with his friends down at the movie theater and that meant we didn't have to worry that they would try to mess with us, and Isaac's grandpa had invited us all over for some space spaghetti. Isaac's grandpa is the coolest guy ever! He may be old, but he is the best kind of old . . . he's space old. Isaac's grandpa used to be an astronaut. I mean a real life, go into a rocket ship, fly to the moon, do spacewalks, collect rocks (according to his grandpa astronauts collect a lot of rocks), wear a space suit, float in space, see other planets, ASTRONAUT! His name is Roger, which he thinks is funny because I guess a hundred years ago or so they had these phones that people would talk back and forth on and when they wanted to say, "I hear you" they would instead say "roger that."

So Isaac's grandpa tells us people used to call him on these phones and always say, "roger that, Roger." I guess the moral of that story is that all old people have dumb stories they think are funny . . . even when they are astronauts. Sue, Isaac, and I have to put up with those to get to the really cool space stories.

A couple times a year Isaac's grandpa will make us his famous space spaghetti, and those are the best days because as soon as we finish the space spaghetti he will tell us a new space adventure story. The last one he told us was about how he threw up in the spaceship once and because there was no gravity it was floating all over the place for days. Sue got sick two weeks later and threw up in a bag, and we all stared at it imaging what it would be like to see it floating around our heads. So gross!

"What do you think your grandpa is going to tell us this time, Isaac? Has he given you any hints?" I asked.

"I don't know, all I know is it is going to be good! He's been working on the space spaghetti all day," Isaac replied.

We all know that the space spaghetti is just normal spaghetti with extra meatballs that Isaac's grandpa calls asteroids, but we never say anything because it's obvious how much Roger likes us all pretending the spaghetti is special. Plus, we don't want to be rude.

Isaac slowed his bike and stopped. We all stopped next to him, and he turned his head really slowly to us and whispered, "Maybe today he'll tell us about the aliens."

Nobody said anything. We have been patiently

waiting for years for Isaac's grandpa to tell us about the aliens. We know they are up there, that's a given, and it's only a matter of time before Roger tells us about them. Isaac and I made eye contact and got that super excited look, then we turned to Sue and instantly knew something was wrong. She was just staring at the ground. We were talking about aliens right then and that means business and for Sue to not be acting excited, well, something was up.

I decided to try to find out and in an attempt at being subtle asked, "What's wrong with you, Sue?" I know, not exactly my best attempt at the art of subtleness.

She looked up and made eye contact with me and then started crying, "He's gone! He's gone, and I don't know where!"

Isaac and I both jumped off our bikes and put our

arms around her. That's what Super Friends do when one of us has a breakdown.

"I didn't know how to tell you about Ralph. It seems like 'little kid' stuff, but to me it's more than that. Ralph helps me."

"Who's Ralph?" Isaac asked.

Have you ever had a friend about to share a HUGE secret with you? You know how their eyes get this super intense look, forceful almost, and they stare at you with this deepness, like life is about to change once you hear this? Well, that is exactly how Sue looked right then. She slowly opened her mouth, Isaac and I raised onto our tippy toes, leaning closer . . . closer . . . closer. And then the words starting shooting out of Sue's mouth.

"When I was little, I mean can't ride a bike yet little, I was sitting in my room crying. My dad came in, and he rushed to me and said, 'What's wrong, Sue Baby?'

I looked up at him and realized I didn't know what was wrong. I just needed to cry, I guess. So I told him the truth."

"Dad, sometimes girls just cry.' He stood up tall and just stared at me like I was an alien. He stood there for what felt like an hour, and then without saying a word he turned around and left the room. Two days later I came home from school and went to put my book bag in my room. On my bed was a stuffed octopus with a note. I touched the octopus. He was soft, and I totally liked the way he felt."

Then I picked up the note:

Sue. Crying is okay. Dads don't get girls sometimes, but Ralph here always does. So when you need to cry, hold his crying leg and let it out. When you get angry, grab Ralph's angry leg and slam him against the bed. It's okay, Ralph is there for you. When you are sick, hold Ralph's sick leg, and he will comfort you. Happy, sad, excited, or mad, Ralph is always here for you.

Isaac and I looked at Sue. She thought we were judging her. Her face got defensive, and she almost shouted, "What are you guys thinking? You better not make fun of me, or I'll call you both Worm until the day you die!"

Isaac and I said it almost at the exact same time,

"I wish I had a Ralph."

Sue held our arms and whispered, "Sorry, I thought you were going to make fun of me."

Isaac said, "No way."

"So what happened to him?" I asked

"I don't know. He's missing. I searched the entire house. I looked in my dad's truck, under seats, I checked the washing machine, the back yard. He's gone."

We all huddled around not knowing exactly what our next move should be. Isaac looked at his watch and told us that if we still wanted space spaghetti we needed to head to his house. After we discussed it we decided that was the best course of action. Sue wanted something to take her mind off of the missing Ralph, and I thought that maybe we could ask Isaac's grandpa for some help searching.

Normally I do my very best to avoid asking for

help from grownups, but I have to admit to myself there are times when adults actually are helpful—though it is extremely rare, and I mean *extremely*. Most of the time they just ask you silly questions you already have asked yourself. For instance, when you have misplaced your favorite toy they will ask, "Where was the last place you saw it?" Like we kids don't have the brain power to think to look in the last place we were playing with something. I mean *come on*.

But if there was anyone who could help us locate where Ralph had disappeared to, I thought it could be Isaac's grandpa. He was an astronaut after all!

CHAPTER 2

We parked our bikes in Isaac's yard and opened the door.

The smell of the space spaghetti hit our noses like a

runaway train. It smelled *sooooo* good! I know it's just

regular spaghetti, but sometimes I wonder if maybe there

isn't some special ingredient he puts in that comes from

space. Like Moon Powdered Garlic or Crumpled Venus

Leaves or Dried Extra-Terrestrial Brains. I hope it's not

dried alien brains, but even if it is . . . I would eat it. It's

that good!

"Hi Isaac, Sue . . . Worm." Okay, prepare yourself

for the awful truth. Todd once told Isaac's grandpa that I

like the name Worm. I know it's awful, beyond awful

really. I was like four years old and didn't really know that Todd was totally the worst brother in the entire galaxy so I nodded my head. Ever since that day Isaac's grandpa has called me Worm, and I really don't have the heart to tell him to stop. Besides he might think it's rude, and I know that somewhere in his house there is a death ray gun, and I don't ever want to make Isaac's grandpa mad.

We found him hovering over a large metal pan in the kitchen. Steam was rising out of it, and it wasn't hard imaging it as a witch's cauldron and that some great magic spell was getting released into the world. Isaac's grandpa had a long wooden spoon, and he was slowly swirling around the sauce (witch's brew). He looked up as we walked into the kitchen and smiled. Immediately the vision of a witch was broken. Isaac's grandpa has one of the best, most friendly smiles in the world. Almost all grandpas have the best smiles, but there was something even more special about Roger's.

"Hi, Grandpa!"

"Hi, Roger."

"Hi, Roger, the space spaghetti smells out of this world!" I said, not even realizing the pun I had just made.

Roger smiled even wider and laughed. "Good one, Worm. I hope it tastes as good as it smells, and your timing is perfect. Isaac, set the table, and let's start eating. Today I have a very special story to tell. I think it's one you've been waiting to hear."

We all just stood there. We slowly turned our heads and mouthed "aliens." For a second I almost completely forgot about the missing Ralph, but I wouldn't be a Super Friend if I totally forgot about things like that. Still I couldn't believe the words were coming out of my mouth when I turned back to Isaac's grandpa and said, "Actually, Roger, we need to tell you a story today. Something happened to Sue, and we need your help."

"Well, that sounds important, and an old man's stories can wait. Hurry with those plates, Isaac, we need to get to the bottom of this."

Moments later we all sat at the table eating the best space spaghetti ever made. It was more than obvious that he was planning on telling us about the aliens today; no one makes spaghetti this good without planning something huge. Someday I will probably ask a girl to marry me . . . as gross as that sounds. I don't ever think about it, but my mom apparently does. She never stops talking about the day "I GET MARRIED." I'm half convinced she has already arranged it with some other mom out there.

I can just see her scheming it out at the grocery store. No doubt all the moms are there; they probably have some secret room in the back that has been built just for them all to sit around and plan out their children's lives together. Gosh knows they go to the grocery store often enough. No one buys that much groceries, and I can tell you first hand there is never anything to eat in our house, so she is doing something other than buying food. I hope Tiffany Green's mom isn't there.

Tiffany is like the worst. I mean worst. She always raises her hand every time our teacher asks a question, she brings her apples and everything. Who brings apples to a teacher anymore? That is so 1990s. And Tiffany follows me around on the playground always trying to get me to talk to her. Once I came around the corner, and she was there with three other annoying girls, and I heard her saying "Hank is sooooo *cute!*" I turned around as quick as I could and ran faster than a cheetah to Isaac. The whole time I was running I thought I could hear their footsteps behind me, like lions trying to capture a gazelle in the wild.

Anyway, all that to say that if the time to ask a girl (it *will not* be Tiffany Green!) to marry me actually comes around I will make spaghetti that tastes as good as this to do it. I wonder if Isaac's grandpa will let me borrow some of his secret ingredients.

As we shoveled the space spaghetti into our mouths, Isaac's grandpa started asking us questions.

"So what is the story you want to tell me?"

We looked at Sue, and she told Isaac's grandpa about the missing octopus. She left out the crying stuff and the note her dad had written, and I didn't blame her. Some things are yours to keep, and it's completely up to you who you want to share them with.

"And now he's missing?" Isaac's grandpa asked.

"Yes. It's been two days now, and I can't find him

anywhere," Sue replied.

"Where was the last place you remember seeing Ralph?" Oh no, he was asking the standard grownup questions. I thought to myself that this was going to be a great waste of time. You could see the look on Sue and Isaac's face that they were thinking the exact same thing, but before Sue even answered Roger said, "That's a dumb question. I'm sure you already thought about that." Whew, score one for Isaac's grandpa.

"Let me ask you this though, Sue," and he leaned toward us as he asked, "Is there anyone who would want to *take* Ralph?"

Sue quickly responded. "No. Who would want to take my stuffed octopus? I'm the only one he has any special meaning to."

Isaac's grandpa leaned back in his chair, "Hmmmm . . . let's think about that for a second. Isaac,

Worm, Sue, is there anyone out there that might find it fun to take something that you had a special attachment to? Someone a little older that might think it's downright funny to mess with you guys for no reason, to take something you like and hide it, to steal your—"

We interrupted him all at the same time, yelling out the name of our most detested enemy. The one person in this world who only receives joy at the sadness of others. The bully on the block. The degrader of souls. The Worm Catcher. "TODD!" We screamed. And then we jumped out of our seats and ran to our bikes.

"To the Secret Hideout!" Sue shouted, and we peddled as fast as we could.

In the kingdom of kids there are four places that are sacred above all others. Four places where the mere mention of them can cause awe and wonder. They are The Fort, The Clubhouse, The Treehouse, and The

Secret Hideout. Within the sanctuary of these mystical places time stands still and all the best schemes and plans ever laid out happen. There is no doubt that within some fort somewhere the skateboard was invented, the pogo stick was given life, and the swimming pool diving board was created. When faced with a mystery Sue knew exactly where we would find our answers, for within the walls of The Secret Hideout the mysteries of all mankind could be solved and within the safety of our private lair we would be able to not only determine exactly how Todd had stolen Ralph, but also the best way to bring Ralph back to safety.

We paddled fast and furious down the street and came to a screeching halt outside Sue's backyard. There was a wooden gate there with a rope that you had to pull to open the latch. Isaac went to the front of the lawn. It was his job to signal if anyone was watching. He would hoot like an owl three times if someone was in sight and bark like a dog seven times if it was safe. My job was to count the barks and then signal to Sue it was safe to pull the rope. Once she pulled the rope we had exactly five seconds to run behind the fence and close the gate. Isaac had the hardest job of all because making it to the gate in five seconds from the front yard was tough. He had to haul. Four times he hadn't made it.

The first time Isaac didn't make it in the required timeframe we were at a loss as what to do. From then on we made a secret password that only we knew. *Jumping Beans In My Pants.* If Isaac got caught he had to utter that phrase, and we would open the gate up for exactly three seconds before closing it again. When it comes to Secret Hideouts, you can never be too safe.

I listened closely for Isaac's cue. It took a minute before he made any noise, which was good. That meant

Isaac was really looking hard. In all the years of the Secret Hideout there had never been as important a moment as this. Sue had taken hold of the rope; she was ready. Suddenly a dog started barking. . . or actually Isaac started barking, but he was so good at barking it was hard to know if it was him or a real dog. That's why we needed exactly seven barks. Bark. Bark. Bark. Bark. Bark. Bark. I got in my sprinter's stance. Sue had her hand on the rope. . . . Nothing . . . nothing . . . then: Bark. She pulled down on the rope with all her strength, the latch let go, she pushed the gate open, and I was right behind her. There were three seconds left, and BAM! Isaac was there.

We closed the gate and looked at astonishment at Isaac. He had never moved that fast before. We each gave him a nod of admiration. He was breathing hard, but returned with a nod back at us. We listened over Isaac's gasping to make sure no one was on the move. We looked up around the gate prepared for any number of ninjas to suddenly appear. Nothing, we were safe. We walked further into Sue's backyard on our way to the Secret Hideout.

To understand our Secret Hideout you first have to understand Sue's dad. He built it. And he built the world's greatest Secret Hideout ever. You see, Sue's dad must not have been told that Sue was a girl or if he had been he forgets all the time. His first gift to her was a football. His second a G.I. Joe action figure. Sue says he tries really hard, but just can't quite get himself to understand that a Monster High doll is a perfectly acceptable gift. So before Sue's fifth birthday she decided to help him out. He was standing on their backyard porch at the grill making hamburgers and hotdogs. She tugged on his shirt, and he looked down and she said, "Hi, Daddy. I'm turning five in a few months. I don't want a

BB gun, but I know that you're allergic to the girl aisle in the store. So how about you build me a playhouse in the backyard?"

In Sue's mind she could see this beautiful pink house with white shutters that she could play tea parties and fairy princess in. Sue's dad looked out at the backyard for a long time. The hamburgers and hot dogs started burning while slowly he started to get this huge grin on his face. Sue walked away feeling so happy. When she turned five, Sue's dad made her put on a blindfold, and he took her to the backyard. She took it off as he shouted, "Surprise!" But there was nothing there. The grass where she had envisioned her elaborate playhouse with its perfect white shutters was nowhere to be seen. Her dad took his finger and placed it under her chin and pushed her eyes up and then she saw it, hidden in the large trees way in the back of her yard. She screamed with delight and moments later had both Isaac and me over to see it.

It is the world's best Secret Hideout because it takes elements of all four of the best kid places on earth and has them all in one.

It is part treehouse, with wooden planks nailed on the back of the tree to climb up to a trap door that has a padlock on it. Only Isaac, Sue, and I know the combination.

It is part fort because it has four windows on each side with wooden shutters that can be locked shut so no one can get inside.

It is part clubhouse with a wooden table and wooden chairs right in the middle. There is even a place in one corner that has glued down cushions so you can lay down and be comfortable. Perfect for playing card games like Crazy 8's and Old Maid.

Her dad built it way up high, deep in the branches

and painted it dark green so if you didn't know it was there, you would never even be able to see it! In the years that have passed we have added some very important elements. It now has a rope ladder that can be hoisted down as well as a plank that you can walk off of and land dead center in the trampoline she got last year for her birthday.

Within moments we had scaled the rope and unlocked the trap door. We had to work the combination padlock twice because our hands were slick with sweat and our minds were focused on the dilemma of the missing Ralph. Once inside we huddled around the table. Isaac started us off by telling us we should all list out the facts in the case of the missing octopus. We decided that each of us would share one fact, and then the next person would share the next one. Sue went first.

"Ralph was last seen in my house. He was sitting

on the couch, where I had left him the night before while I was watching a movie with my dad."

I went next. "My stinky older brother loves to torture us, and if he knew about Ralph he would make it his lifelong goal to steal him and inflict horror upon horror on the poor octopus."

Sue gasped, and Isaac whispered to me, "You may want to take it easy on the 'inflicting horrors' stuff." Then he said louder, "We know that if Todd broke into your house, that would be illegal, and as far as we know Todd hasn't started breaking the law . . . yet. So, I think we can assume that if he got in your house he used his sneakiness to get in."

Sue said, "I should ask my dad if Todd was in the house that morning Ralph went missing."

"Great idea," I said.

Sue then went over to one of the walls and picked

up the phone. Yes, that's correct. There was a REAL phone in the Secret Hideout. I told you! It is the coolest hideout ever! It's bright red and looks like the phone the president would use when he wants to call a missile strike. She picked it up and dialed her dad. He was at work, but she called his cell phone number, and he picked up immediately. She put it on the speakerphone option so we could all hear.

"Everything okay, Sue Baby?" Sue's dad always calls her Sue Baby. I don't think he has ever just called her Sue. Sometimes I wonder if that might be a little awkward when she is older, but Sue seems to like it, and that's all that's important.

"Yes, Dad."

"How was lunch with Roger?"

"It was great, but hey, Dad, I wanted to ask you something?"

"Yes, what is it, Sue Baby?"

"Was Todd in the house a couple days ago?"

"Why do you want to know, sweetheart?" Isaac and I looked at each other. We hadn't thought about the potential for this question! We should have been ready; it was a standard adult question, but we had blown it. We mouthed to Sue, "Abort! Abort!"

But Sue was way ahead of us, as casual as can be she replied, "No big reason. It's just that Hank is missing a toy and apparently Todd took it from him. Hank wondered if maybe Todd had hidden it over here. You know . . . boys and all."

Sue's dad laughed. "Boys will be boys. Yes, Todd was in the house two days ago. He said that he was locked out of his house and that he needed to use the bathroom. As far as I know he went straight to the bathroom and left immediately after. Tell Hank to check in there. If it was anything like my brothers and me, it may be in the toilet tank. All you have to do is lift the lid to see." Her dad laughed some more and then after a quick exchange of I love yous, have a nice days, and see you laters, Sue hung up.

After running into the bathroom to check if Ralph was indeed hidden in the murky depths that exists behind the toilet tank and finding nothing. It was official. Beyond any reasonable doubt, Todd had taken Ralph. We walked back to the Secret Hideout all the while wondering what poor fate that eight-legged friend of Sue's has endured since being captured by Todd the Destroyer of Dreams.

"Ohh Ralph . . ." Sue sighed, hiding her head in the palms of her hands.

Isaac said, "He's a POW. A true prisoner of war." They were giving up hope. I wouldn't let them.

"People, people. Stop. If I gave up every time Todd took his brand of vengeance out on me, I would be long gone from this world." I stood up from my chair. "If I laid down every time my horrible older brother ripped a toy from my hand, I would be lost like some castaway doomed to walk a lonely island, forever toyless." I raised my hands. I was in the moment. I could feel my troops rallying to me: Isaac's head was raised, Sue was listening, her hands now becoming fists.

"If I turned my back in failure at every worm that I ate, or that was thrown on me, or that I woke up next to . . . then you would be just in calling me Worm. BUT I AM NOT A WORM!" I looked at Sue. "Are you a worm, Sue?"

"*No!*" She shouted.

I turned to Isaac. "Are you a worm, Isaac?"

"*Nooooo!*" He shouted. They were both out of

their chairs now. We walked to the window and stared out at Sue's house. We couldn't see my yard from here, her house blocked it from view, but within our own minds it stood there. We could see through the roof, through the walls and in our minds eyes we could see exactly where we should begin our attack. Todd's Room.

CHAPTER 3

My older brother Todd's room has been off limits to every family member for as long as my brain can remember. I haven't seen the inside of it in years, and for all I know it is covered in vines and plant life like some lethal rain forest jungle. Without question there are man-eating Venus flytraps the size of small automobiles and probably tarantulas that obey his every command like the evil villain that he is. Sometimes at night, if I creep down the hall toward his door and if I listen closely I can even hear the exotic cries of some long forgotten reptile and the sound of bats flapping in the foul air that his room must reek of.

To even attempt to enter into Todd's domain was to be willing to give up your very life, because if we were caught . . . I shuddered at the mere thought of what would happen. Isaac broke the silence with a whisper. "This will be the most dangerous mission of our lives."

Sue answered back. "We should write our wills before we head over." And she walked to a small box near the table and pulled out markers and paper. Normally we just use that paper to draw silly pictures, but today it would be used to declare who our belongings should go to in case we were captured and killed while attempting to free Ralph from Todd's room.

We all sat down and began writing our wills. I made sure to use lots of legal terms like, whom, hereby, and other stuff that I have seen lawyers say on movies. Here was mine:

In the event of my death, I hereby want

1. *All of my action figures to be distributed, one each, at my funeral to all the people who showed up to cry and bemoan my passing.*

2. *All the meals that I will not be able to eat hence forward, I want to go to the hungry children of Africa, whom my mom tells me never have enough to eat. I have had to finish my plate 347 times for you children, now you can have the whole thing.*

3. *My skateboard and bike should be donated to the Smithsonian Museum where they shall be displayed to future generations to know what type of transportation kids today had available to them.*

4. *To my cousin Jimmy who lives in the state of Idaho I hereby give my rubber band gun and all my Nerf toys.*

5. Everything else should be burned in a great Viking

Pyre at my burial. May it light up the sky and

provide hope for every kid called Worm.

6. I also would like a canon at my funeral and 20

archers that shoot flame arrows.

Once we each completed our wills is was time to come up with our strategy on freeing Ralph. First we knew we needed a recon mission. I had recently watched an awesome action movie called *NightFire 6* where a secret group of army rangers had to go to a remote village full of bad guys, but they were under strict orders not to "engage" the enemy. They had to go ninja style and sneak into the base, look around, take some pictures of the bad guys' plans, and get out without be seen. It was called a recon or reconnaissance mission. After about 30 minutes of back and forth we had our plan. It was foolproof.

First, we would come in the back door. I have a glass patio door that leads to my backyard. I can see inside the house and make sure it's all clear before we enter. I would open the door, do a tuck and roll army move, and end up behind the couch. I would signal it was safe, and then Sue would do the same roll move, then Isaac. Then we would split up and find safe recon points throughout my house. This was the part of the plan that we had the most back and forth about. I was all for the splitting up because that's what they did during the recon mission in *Nightfire 6*, but Isaac was totally against it. He had just watched a horror movie called *Don't Open the Door* about vampires, and all the people had split up and the vampires had eaten them one by one. Sue was the deciding vote, and she couldn't make up her mind, so we did what we always do when we run into these types of problems. We settled it over rock, paper, scissors.

I threw rock down, and Isaac went scissors. It was decided and there was no more room for argument. Rock, paper, scissors is by far the best way to settle any argument between people. I have often wondered why leaders of countries don't do the same thing. I think it would stop a lot of wars.

After splitting up we would all find vantage points to be able to signal each other in the event of hostile enemies, otherwise known as Todd and his friends. Our signal would be this cool lighting code system that we had learned about at school when studying the American Revolution. Apparently there was this guy named Paul Revere, and it was his job to watch if the Red Coats were coming. He would light one lantern if they were coming by land and two lanterns if they were coming by sea. Sue was the one who remembered it best and she came up with the idea that if Todd or his friends entered the house the person who saw them would run to the nearest light switch and flick it. Once if they came in through the front door, twice if they came in from the back door, and to be safe we decided three times in case Todd tried to sneak in through a window.

The next step of the plan was to infiltrate the upstairs and sneak into Todd's room. Isaac wanted to be the brave one and go into the room. Sue then said she should because it was her fault we were in this mess to begin with and if someone was going to get captured and killed it should be her. But I settled it by saying that Todd was my older brother and ultimately it was my responsibility to put myself in harm's way. I would go in, and I would go in alone. Isaac and Sue would be in charge of watching the stairs when I entered. In the event that some animal tried to eat me or I fell into some fiendishly clever trap of Todd's, Isaac would be the first to come in to save me, followed by Sue. If we saw Ralph, we would grab him and run. It was the perfect plan—or so we thought.

We left the Secret Hideout and ran across the street to my house. Within seconds we were safe at the patio door. I went up and looked through while Sue and Isaac stayed hidden behind some bushes. The house was darker than normal as if it knew what we were about to do and was trying to help us by creating more shadows. I opened the door and went to do my roll. That's when the first thing went wrong.

I mistimed the roll and ended up slamming my back into an end table, and it started shaking back and forth causing the glass lamp that was on it to start to fall. I thought for sure it was going to hit the ground and shatter into a million pieces when out of nowhere Sue appeared and caught the lamp just inches from the floor.

"Whew!" I said to her.

"Shh!" she said. Then Isaac rolled behind her. His roll was perfect. Sue and I both stared at him for a second. Sometimes your friends do stuff that really astonishes you and you feel so lucky to be able to call them friends. At that moment that's exactly how Sue and I felt about Isaac. No doubt someday he would be an astronaut just like his grandpa and fight evil aliens and probably save the world from being turned into mindless alien slave zombies.

Sue put the lamp back on the end table, and we all huddled behind the couch. We counted to ten, and then all of us jumped up together and ran in different directions. Sue headed toward the kitchen, Isaac made his way to the den, and I went straight for the stairs. I was halfway up when the second thing went wrong, but I didn't learn about it until later. Maybe you have already thought about our light switch plan and realized the error we had made. You see, when I'm upstairs I can't see the kitchen light switch being turned on and off. So when Sue tried to alert me that Todd was *already* home and in the kitchen making himself a sandwich I never saw the lights flicker so I just went up the stairs, took the 15 steps, and opened the door into . . . Todd's lair.

I opened the door and closed it as fast as I could. It took all of my courage to be in there, and I didn't want the door open so I could easily chicken out. I was still holding the handle and staring at the door. I closed my eyes and counted to ten as calmly as I could, then I slowly turned around and looked into the room that my older brother called home. It was disgusting. The smell alone could kill a baby. I swear you could see a fuming green gas floating in the air. There were clothes everywhere, some scattered all by themselves, but most built into large piles. It may have been a trick of the eye, but I would lay my hand on a bible and tell a judge that I witnessed two of the piles move.

I took one step into the room and heard a scampering, like some giant rat was on the move. I jumped back to the door and waited another ten seconds. I had no way of knowing it, but directly beneath me in the kitchen Todd had seized hold of Sue and was asking what in the heck she was doing flickering the light switch.

I took another step into the room and this time there was no noise. I took another step and then I saw *it*. It wasn't Ralph . . . it was something I could only have imagined in my deepest, darkest nightmares. I was drawn to it, like a siren whispering my name in a sea fog. My face almost bumped right into the glass enclosure before I stopped moving. Before me, standing about four feet tall was . . . a worm farm. Housed inside were hundreds of worms moving within a tunnel system that they had created all by themselves. The glass allowed you to see their every move, every slither, every wiggle and turn.

It captivated my entire mind and long unanswered questions were being answered. I now knew exactly where Todd got his worms, how he seemed to have an endless supply. He was their king, reigning over an entire colony of worms. He had leaves and apple cores sitting at the top of the farm, and you could watch worms eating. I knew that worms loved to eat the fruit that we throw away, but I had never seen them actually do it. It was fascinating. I don't know how long I stood there, but I learned later that while I gazed upon Todd's worms Isaac had also been captured by Todd. Apparently he heard Todd asking Sue questions and tried to sneak by the kitchen to come warn me when Todd saw him. My brother Todd can strike faster than a rattlesnake when he's mad and like a gunshot he had grabbed hold of both Sue and Isaac.

Inside his lair I had just come out of the worm trance and was realizing that I needed to get back to the mission when suddenly I was distracted again. On his desk next to the worm farm was a composition notebook, like the kind that can be seen by the pile at any middle school in America. Normally I would have just passed right by this notebook without a further thought, but written in black marker was a title that demanded my attention: *Big Plans for Little Worm*. And directly below the title appeared to be a drawing of a worm wearing my favorite hat, in fact it wasn't hard to see that the drawing was supposed to be me as a worm.

I opened the notebook to a random page and there were lists of horrendous things that apparently Todd planned on doing to me. Some of the list had been struck through and I quickly realized this represented

things Todd had already done.

Hide dirt in Worms chocolate milk

Put a worm in shoe

Add worms to his cereal box

Give him worms for Christmas present

Tell him his real mom is a worm from outer space

Give Worm and his loser friends cookies with dirt
hidden in them

Put dirt in his meatloaf

Crumb. We just had meatloaf last week.

Apparently I have now eaten dirt involuntarily 38 times. I

flipped the pages and it was more of the same. List upon

list of horrors my older brother wanted to do to me. In

some places there were drawings, one of which I was

being eaten alive by a giant worm that had a saddle, and Todd was riding it. I had to get this book to my mom! I no sooner had that thought then the worst possible thing imaginable happened. The door opened.

I dropped the book as quickly as I could and turned to look for a hiding place, but it was too late. He stood there in the door, like some great super villain returned from conquering a planet. In his right hand was Isaac, looking like he was about to cry. In his left hand was Sue. She was choosing to go with a defiant look. His hideous mouth opened and the words that came out of it scared me to the deepest recesses of my soul.

"Oh, Worm . . . big mistake."

CHAPTER 4

Moments later all three of us Super Friends were forced into the backyard where we were made to stand with our backs against the wall. Before we had left Todd's room he had grabbed a white pillowcase that looked full of stuff. I didn't know what was in that pillowcase, but I feared I was about to find out. I grabbed Sue's hand in my left and Isaac's in my right. All three of us were trembling. Todd placed the pillowcase on the ground in front of him, and then he began pacing back and forth.

"So, Worm, I believe I have just discovered you in my room. Is that correct?"

I didn't reply. Years of torture had prepared me

for this moment. I long knew that any response would be used against me. Silence was my only companion.

"Yes. Yes that is correct," he answered himself, taking long strides as he paced. He brought his hand to his chin.

"I guess it was only a matter of time before you wormed your way into my room and went through my stuff. Now I know I've told you countless times that going in my room was a big no-no, isn't that correct, Worm?"

My mouth almost betrayed me and said yes, but thankfully at the last moment I was able to regain control of my lips and keep them closed.

"And now, here we are. You have disobeyed a direct order from me, your older brother. Your highest authority."

"You are not his highest authority! His mom is!"

Oh, Sue. She didn't understand. A rookie mistake. Engaging a superior enemy in a battle of wits was exactly what he wanted. Todd smiled.

"Don't worry, Sue *Baby*," he knew what Sue's dad called her and used it against her, "I'm going to teach you that I am indeed the highest authority. For too long I've let Worm here hang out with you bothersome little ants. It's time to teach you a lesson." Sue quivered. She turned to me for help. I looked away. There was nothing I could do. I just squeezed her hand hoping that in our last moments any remaining strength I had could be passed to my two Super Friends. Maybe that would grant me some brownie points in heaven, and I would be forgiven for all the bad things I have said about Tiffany Green, but with my luck some distant deceased relative of hers would be in charge of admissions in heaven.

Todd kept pacing as he said, "What to do? What

to do?" He paused, bringing his hand to his chin, portraying the actions of someone deep in thought, but I knew better. Todd was incapable of deep thought.

"I think . . ." And he stopped dead in his tracks. "Yes. *Yes!* I think I know exactly what to do." He turned to us. We leaned back, attempting to push the wall behind us over so we could make more room between us and my horrible older brother.

"You guys are best friends, right?" He said this almost like a normal person, and except for the glint in his eye you could almost have mistaken the question as coming from someone who actually cared.

It was Isaac's turn to say something stupid. "No, we're *Super Friends* and nothing you can do will ever-"

Todd moved fast. He was inches from Isaac, who very smartly shut his moth. The stench of Todd's breath that close to Isaac's face almost knocked him to his knees.

"Well, thank you Isaiah." Todd knew Isaac's name, he was trying to bait him into saying something else, but Isaac was a quick learner and kept his trap shut.

"I would hate to misrepresent this band of misfits. *Super Friends*, huh? Super Friends it is. Now I'm sure you guys, being the amazing friends you are—excuse me, the *Super* friends you are—have completed the ritual of true friends?"

He looked to us, meeting each one of us in the eyes at the same time. I have no clue how he was able to do that, but one of Todd's Super Villain powers is the ability to simultaneously look at multiple objects at once without going cross-eyed. In this way he is able to mess with me at the dinner table while still being able to know exactly where my mom is looking and therefore knowing when he has to stop before she will see him. It is a remarkable power, and I'm sure he traded his soul for it long ago in some forgotten alley.

"Come on now, I'm just asking a simple question. Worm, have you and your *pals* done the ritual of true friends?" We turned toward each other briefly asking each other without words if anyone knew what in the heck he was talking about. I turned back to my older brother and shook my head no.

He threw his hands in the air and said loudly, "We can't have *that!* You guys aren't real friends, surely not *SUPER* friends without completing the ritual. I can help. Let's see here . . ." and he took his grimy hands and went searching in the pillow case. "Yes, yes . . . we'll need these." And he threw out three long strips of what looked like parts of a sheet. "Oh, and we'll have to have these." And out came a mason jar full of some type of dirt, but he placed it far enough behind him that I couldn't really see what it was.

"And last of all, it's not a proper ritual without *this*." And out came a pack of colored markers.

Our imaginations went into overdrive as we tried to determine just what type of death was headed our way. Would he tie us up with the sheets and then shove the markers into our nose until they penetrated our brains? Would he make us eat the dirt in the mason jar while stabbing us with the marker points until we died?

As we thought out the hundreds of ways Todd would use those objects to end our existence we watched him pick them up from the ground and move toward us. He went to Sue first and tied the strips of sheet around her eyes. Ahh . . . blindfold. Yep, that makes sense. At least this way we wouldn't see the end coming. We would go out like some line of people in a firing squad. Next was my turn, and I heard Isaac fight back a little until he made an "uumphh" noise. No doubt Todd had given him a gut shot.

"And now, we must start the ritual of true friends with the ceremonial drawing on skin." I felt the marker make contact on my face. He was not gentle with the marker, and my only consolation was that it would all be over soon. Once he was done with me I heard him move to Isaac and then to Sue.

We could hear him step back from us, and then he started laughing his hideous laugh. It sounds like a lawnmower breaking.

"And now, repeat after me. I am a *true friend*." None of us said anything. "I SAID, REPEAT AFTER ME. I AM A TRUE FRIEND."

We all started chanting, "I am a true friend."

Todd cried out, "LOUDER. The gods of friendship can't hear you."

"I AM A TRUE-" and then it happened. As my mouth was opened to loudly shout out *friend* a worm was shoved into my mouth. Then his smelly, disgusting hand was covering my mouth forcing me to swallow the worm. I fought with all my might. I tried to spit, to push the worm out of my mouth with my tongue, but Todd was too strong. There was only one option. I swallowed.

I fell to my knees ashamed of what had just happened. Todd could be heard laughing in the distance. I reached up and removed the blindfold. Sue was throwing up in the grass. Isaac was staring at the sky, perhaps his mind had failed him and he would be forced to roam the earth forever lost in a cloud of insanity.

Sue looked at Todd who was opening the patio door, still laughing and she shouted, "GIVE ME RALPH BACK!"

Todd stopped laughing and looked at her. "Who

is Ralph?"

"Don't play dumb with me. I'll eat as many worms as you want, just give me my stuffed octopus back."

Todd's face gave it away. He had no clue what she was talking about. You could see him devising a plan, and suddenly he said, "Oh yeah. That Ralph. I'll give you Ralph back after you eat twenty worms."

But it was no good. We all knew the truth. Todd had never taken Ralph. We shuffled back to the Secret Hideout. We didn't say one word to each other until we were safe inside. We lay down on the cushions, all of us shocked by what happened. Moments turned into hours and without our ever noticing it had turned dark outside. It was time to go home. My mom would be back from work, Sue's dad was probably about to come into the driveway any minute, and Isaac's grandpa would want to know what happened. We got up, looked at each other, and Isaac led us in saying, "We never talk about this to anyone."

I replied, "We carry it to our graves."

Sue said, "Forever it is our secret." She hesitated and then said, "But if he doesn't have Ralph . . . who does?"

Isaac and I had nothing to offer so we just hunched our shoulders. We left the Secret Hideout and started back home. Sue walked us to the driveway, and we were saying goodbye as her dad pulled in.

"Hey, Sue Baby. Hello, Isaac. Hello, Hank." We waived back halfheartedly, and then Sue's dad reached behind his back and pulled out a stuffed octopus. "Look who I have, Sue Baby!" She ran and grabbed Ralph. "I noticed the other day he was getting pretty dirty so I took him to the cleaners."

Sue turned to us smiling. It was a great day . . .

well, except for the worm eating.

THE SCHOOL PLAY DISASTER

By the middle of summer we found ourselves staring at each other a lot in the Secret Hideout. Isaac's grandpa had not started another vat of space spaghetti, leaving me to further conclude that he was waiting for more ingredients to arrive from Saturn or some exotic planet so far removed from our galaxy it is labeled QR14-H or something like that. We had to memorize the planets in our solar system last year in school, and I have no clue who names these things. Mercury, Neptune? Are you kidding me? It should be something way cooler than that. If I was going to name a planet I would go with Xtremous or Planet Skullbreaker or Pirate Planet.

Board games and the like were out. We had

played Crazy 8's so much that the mere mention of it would cause intense hives and our brains to explode. We were completely out of water balloons so that was out of the question, though that had been fun while it lasted. This summer's water balloon fight was epic, and we were even able to throw one at Todd and run away without getting caught, but that had happened over two weeks ago. Now there was nothing left but the memory and an occasional torn balloon scrap found laying around in the yard.

It didn't take much to realize we were in danger of the deepest levels of boredom overtaking us. If we weren't careful it would only be a matter of time before one of us started talking about going back to school. No way was I going to let that happen. I had to do something.

"Let's ride our bikes," I said. I have to admit even

though I tried very hard my heart wasn't in it, and neither Isaac nor Sue even looked up.

After moments of silence I tried again this time with more energy. "I think I can beat you in a bike race, Sue."

Sue is the fastest bike racer known to humankind. I have seen her beat every challenger without even breaking a sweat. She's like lightning on a bike, and when she peddles as fast as she can she leaves streaks of fire on the ground behind her tires. My plan in challenging her was to appeal to her competitive side and tease her into racing. It didn't work. She just raised her hand, waving me off like a pesky fly.

I was getting desperate. I was thinking so hard of something, anything that could get us out of this slump before we entered stage five of boredom. If you aren't aware there are exactly five stages of boredom.

Stage One: Slowness of Action

In this stage you will find yourself slow to move. For instance, let's say you are watching TV and a show you don't like comes on. You look for the remote, but to reach it requires getting off the couch. If you decide you would rather just watch the bad show instead of get the remote, you are officially in Stage One.

Stage Two: Repetitive Acts

Stage Two is when your brain enters into boredom itself, and thinking of things to do is nearly impossible. When your brain hits this stage its turns on auto pilot. You can know you are in this stage if you find yourself opening the fridge door over and over again until your mom or dad yells at you to stop. Another telltale sign is that you go in and out of your house again and again.

Stage Three: Destructive Behavior

Stage Three is a kid's last-ditch effort to get their parents to come up with something for them to do. In this stage, a kid will begin to do things they know they shouldn't. Some classic examples are: throwing a ball in the house, shaving the dog, or seeing what happens to silly putty in the microwave.

Stage Four: Paralysis

When a kid hits Stage Four every muscle in their body starts to surrender to boredom. Any movement becomes difficult, and if not treated early it is not unusual to lose all motor function. Playing of any type becomes nearly impossible for someone in Stage Four. I have heard of a case in which a kid was in stage four for so long that his skin liquefied and eventually turned into jelly. For years doctors have been trying to cure Stage Four, but so far have come up empty.

Stage Five: Want to go to School

I won't even write about Stage Five, it's that horrible. And last year Isaac entered Stage Five with over two weeks left of summer. I won't let it happen again this year.

I was thinking of every possible thing on earth that we could do. Veins were popping out of my head. I was in danger of overload when suddenly I discovered long forgotten games were resurfacing. Things that we did when we were younger were surging into my memory banks. I smiled as I recalled when we used to play imaginary kickball in Isaac's front lawn. Sue always hit home runs. I laughed out loud thinking about the time we played on the swings at the park trying so hard to get the swing to go *all* the way around when I fell out of the swing and almost broke every bone in my body. It was so fun. I heard the common theme of every memory: play . . . play . . . play.

Without realizing it I had begun repeating that same word. I was lost in a trance of long ago memories, and I had no clue that Sue and Isaac were hearing me repeat "play" over and over again. The trance was broken when I felt Sue grab hold of me and start shaking me.

"It's okay, Hank. You don't ever have to think about the school play ever again."

Then Isaac said, "Yeah, Hank. It's over man. It's over."

Even though the school play was the last thing on my mind, hearing them saying it brought it all back to the front. Like it had just happened.

Let me tell you about the time I played the Sheriff of Nottingham in *Robin Hood* and ruined the school play.

Like most horrible things it all began simply enough. It was an ordinary day at school, nothing crazy or weird had happened. We had just come back from recess where Brian Ekerson and I had just dominated a game of basketball.

Brian was the best player, and I was arguably the second best so when you put us on the same team it really wasn't fair for anyone else. As I look back on the events of that day I wonder if that basketball victory had something to do with it.

Sometimes when you win big at something you can start to feel a little cocky, and your guard comes down, so maybe when our English teacher Mr. Hopp started talking about the *Robin Hood* play I wasn't as ready as I should have been. Maybe, just maybe, if I had lost that game of basketball I wouldn't have signed up to be in the *Robin Hood* play, and I could have avoided the disaster that followed. Unfortunately for me, I didn't lose that game, and when Mr. Hopp came in and started selling us all on why we wanted to be in the play I bought it.

When Mr. Hopp makes a sales pitch he does it right. We were all sitting in our desks, the excitement of recess still flowed out of each of us filling the air with the aroma of awesome, also known as sweat and playground dirt. He flung open the door. Our heads snapped to the sound, and he entered in a whoosh. He ran to his desk and jumped onto it in a single leap. He was wearing a green hat with a large red feather sticking out of it. He had a quiver of arrows strapped to his back, and in his right hand was a bow and arrow.

"Class, today I welcome you to a time when forests filled the land." He jumped off his desk, landing inches away from Isaac who sat in the front row. "When the greatest of men were forced to hide deep behind the trees because an evil prince ruled the kingdom. Today I invite you to stop being grade-schoolers and take up arms as we fight villainy and protect the poor who are being taxed beyond their means by the rich and beaten by the worst of sheriffs. There are some here sitting in these desks right now who may be maidens in disguise . . ." He paused and looked at Tiffany Green. Ugh, I said to myself.

"There are some here who are a band of Merry Men who stand behind their great leader." Mr. Hopp spread his hand throughout the students. "I can see an evil prince full of greed . . ." and he stared at Brian Ekerson. ". . . and of course right before us is our hero. Our Robin Hood." And he pointed out his hand to Isaac. Isaac was lost in the moment. At the mere mention of being Robin Hood you could see his chest stick out and his chin rise. At that moment in time he had become Robin Hood. He beamed, but I knew better.

Todd had been in *Robin Hood* a few years ago, and my mom had forced me to go and "support my older brother." Todd was one of the Merry Men. It was actually kind of cool; he got a sword and everything. But the thing I remembered most, the thing I knew that Isaac did not, was that Robin Hood had to kiss Maid Marian—and it wasn't hard to read between the lines and see that Mr. Hopp had already cast Tiffany Green for that part. I wanted to warn Isaac right away, but just then Mr. Hopp reached behind his desk and grabbed a bunch of wooden swords and started throwing them out to the class. One landed in my hand and immediately I started sword fighting Sue who sat in the desk to my right.

"So, class, who is with me?"

We were all caught up in the enchantment. Without any thought I shouted alongside my classmates. "We are!" I wish now I could go back in time and grab that sword out of my hand and hit myself on the head. What an idiot I was. If only I had known what was going to happen.

Mr. Hopp passed out a sign-up sheet with parts on it for us to put our names next to if we wanted to play them. By the time it made it to my desk I saw that most of the parts already had been taken. Isaac had signed up for Robin Hood. Tiffany Green for Maid Marian. Poor Isaac, I whispered to myself. I looked for Sue and saw she went for one of the twelve Merry Men parts. Brian was indeed going to be Prince John. There were two slots left for Merry Men, and I thought that would be fun, but I knew Todd had already done that. I didn't want to do a part my stinky older brother had done. Mom would probably try to get me to wear the tights he had worn. I thought Little John would be cool.

Little John was Robin Hood's right hand man, and that meant I could be in all the scenes with Isaac. But when I looked that part was already taken. Friar Tuck was available, and I was thinking of going that route because I knew he didn't have many lines, when suddenly my eyes caught site of the Sheriff of Nottingham. It leaped out of the page, and I thought I could even see a golden sunray surrounding the letters. Again I blame the basketball game. Brian and I had just defeated everyone at recess, and I thought it would be fun to play his evil henchman, the two of us taxing the poor! I signed my name with flair and passed the sheet behind me, feeling kind of smug. I put my hands behind my back and daydreamed of sword fights and armored battles.

The rest of the day was like every other, full of reading out loud, going to the white board and answering math problems in front of everyone, helping pass a note from one person to the next, etc. etc.

When the bell rang Sue, Isaac, and I ran to the bike rack. In seconds we had unpadlocked the bikes and were on our way home. Sue brought up the play telling Isaac he would make a great Robin Hood. None of them knew what I had signed up for since the sign-up sheet had come to them first. I told them I was the Sheriff of Nottingham, and they both thought that was cool.

"I think I kill you, don't I?" said Isaac.

"Yes, you do Mr. Hood. Yes, you do." I looked at him from my bike and saw him smiling to himself. "But I know something you don't know, *Robin*."

Isaac looked over at me.

"You have to kiss Tiffany Green."

His smile melted like wax. "You're lying."

"Sorry, Isaac. No lie. I wanted to tell you before you signed up, but there was no way."

"It's true, Isaac," Sue said. "Robin Hood saves Maid Marian, and then he kisses her."

Isaac looked devastated. Isaac, Sue, and I are

more than friends. If you have ever had a best friend we are that times infinity. And Super Friends never stop having each other's back.

"Isaac, Amigo, Pal of Pals," I started. "You are going to be Robin Hood. How awesome is that?"

Sue jumped in, "Yea, I mean the greatest archer in the universe. You even get to have a bow on stage!"

We looked at Isaac's face and could see that we were getting through. His lips were giving the faintest clues of forming a smile.

Sue continued on, "And you know Tiffany Green doesn't want to kiss you either. It's Hank she wants to smooch until the sun sets."

"I don't think we need to talk about that Sue." I said.

"I mean Isaac, she probably will just peck you for less than a second. Hank is the one she dreams of and writes in her diary about and chases on the playground and…"

"I think he gets the point Sue!" I shouted. I was getting way too close to throwing up.

Isaac patted me on the shoulder. "You guys are right. I'm going to be Robin Hood. Steal from the rich, give to the poor. The world's greatest Hero!"

Once back in our neighborhood we quickly went to the Secret Hideout. We played sword fights, which turned into pirate brigade. Sue got a trampoline last year on her birthday, and her dad built a plank off the Secret Hideout so you can walk right off the plank and land dead center on the trampoline. Isaac made Sue and me both walk off the plank.

When I jump on a trampoline I amaze everyone. I can do front flips, backflips, side flips, and what I call ninja flips. To do a ninja flip you have to get someone to make a double bounce for you.

A double bounce is when someone jumps on the trampoline right before you land on it. This causes the springs to already be activated, and then when you land you get double the spring power. It is dangerously scary to anyone new to trampolining, and I wouldn't advise trying it until you have perfected normal jumps. Once you have the double bounce in place you kick out your right foot with a loud ninja yell, then you go directly into a backflip. You then tuck both feet under you at the last second, use your knees to bounce off the trampoline, and then go into a front flip, kicking out your left foot this time. It's really hard, so if you try it and can't do it, don't feel bad. Neither Isaac nor Sue can, but Sue is getting close, and I bet by next year she has it down.

After we had all walked the plank a few times and I had done about four ninja flips it was starting to get dark so we said goodbye and headed home.

That night I dreamed a strange and crazy sort of nightmare. I found myself dressed as the Sheriff of Nottingham, and Isaac came storming in through a tower window. He pulled out a sword, and I reached for mine, but instead of a sword it was a giant worm. Suddenly from a magic mirror on the wall Todd's face showed up, and he was laughing his hideous laugh. Isaac started laughing as well. He walked closer to me with his sword raised, and he laughed out the words, "Prepare to die, Worm!" and then I woke up just as he was about to stab me.

I was covered in sweat, and as I rolled over to turn the light on, I saw it on the pillow next to me. A worm with a note tied securely around its body. I took off the note and unrolled it. Todd's handwriting, of course. "Hi Worm, your son here missed you. Give little wormie a kiss goodnight. Sweet dreams." Having an older brother is like having the worst case of warts.

That next day at school was boring. We expected to get the script for the play, but nothing arrived. When we asked Mr. Hopp about it, he kind of half smiled, got this crazy eyed look, and said he was still working on it and that we should be prepared for BIG things and he said it in an all capitals kind of way. BIG things.

The only other thing that happened that day was that Sue stepped on an empty soda can in such a way that the can became squished under her shoe and wouldn't let go. It was like it was molded around her foot, and it made this cool metal crushing noise with every step she took. She was able to walk with it on her shoe the entire recess before Mrs. Wallace made her take it off. Mrs. Wallace, otherwise known to us kids as Mrs. Wallace the Walrus, is the meanest teacher that has ever walked the earth. She has made it her sole goal in life to snuff out the fun of children wherever it can be found on this world. I swear that she can actually hear a kid smile and within seconds will arrive to wipe it off their face.

That night I had a ton of homework so there wasn't really any hangout time with Sue and Isaac, which happens sometimes with homework. The whole idea of homework doesn't make sense to me. *Home* should never have the word *work* attached to it. I mean, when you are an adult you go to work and then you go home. They are two different places. Home for an adult is kind of like recess, the place you go to get away from work. Why does school not understand that the same rules should apply for kids? It should just be schoolwork, and that's it.

Another day of school went by and still no script. Weird. When Todd was in *Robin Hood* he had gotten the script the very next day and two weeks later they had put on the play. Every day without the script was less rehearsal time, which really meant less sword fighting time.

I was about to raise my hand and let Mr. Hopp know that enough was enough and to pass out the swords even if the script wasn't ready, when suddenly the fire alarm went off.

The fire alarm is God's gift to schoolchildren. It is the one time at school where chaos rules, where even the teacher can't tell us to stay in our seats. The rules at my school were to get in a line and then go to the nearest exit, which was awesome for my class because the nearest exit was like super close so we got out first. Fresh air! Free from the concrete prison walls that entombed us.

On fire alarm days I think the sun actually shines brighter and the clouds work together to form the coolest dragons. Once all the different classes are out we are supposed to stay in a line with our class, but that never happens. All the teachers get together and start talking among themselves, talking about whatever teachers talk about, probably how to assign more homework without getting in trouble with child labor laws, and once the teachers get together we kids do the same thing.

Isaac, Sue, and I found ourselves toward the back of the group and discovered a large ant hill. I would love to say that we respected the colony of the ants and didn't mess with it, but it is rare to find someone who can walk away from the temptation of stomping on an anthill. I stomped on it first, then Isaac, and last Sue. Within seconds every ant was on the move, and we had been surrounded by a few more classmates. For a while we just stood there in awe of the ants wondering what was going through their little ant brains.

I could just see a soldier ant reporting to the

queen, "Madam Queen. It appears your kingdom has just come under attack from the giants."

"Summon the soldiers! We will not let the giants get away with this! Alert the colony, we go on the march!"

I was deep within my own imagination when I heard *her* behind me. Tiffany Green. To understand just how much her voice annoys me I want you to close your eyes and think of the world's greatest arcade. Full of every video game known to man and all of them completely free. No tokens required. There is even a huge, giant, ball pit for you to jump in. There is a basketball shooting game, and at every corner there are soda fountains dispensing your favorite soda. And every time you roll a skee-ball it goes right into the bull's-eye. Adults aren't allowed in, and you can do whatever you want. Can you see that place? Awesome, right? Now imagine you are walking toward it, just a few steps and you will be inside.

And then it vanishes! Gone. Whoosh. Sayonara. And standing there instead is this blonde haired girl that wears way too much perfume, won't stop talking —ever—and wants to kiss you. That's how much she annoys me.

"Hi, Hank. I hear you are going to be Sheriff of Nottingham. You'll make an incredible sheriff."

I acted like I couldn't hear her.

"It's too bad that you won't be Robin Hood, though. When Robin Hood comes and rescues me from the clutches of Prince John I'll pretend it's you. And when Robin Hood leans in to kiss me Ill pretend it's your lips that-"

Just as I'm about to upchuck my breakfast, Mr. Hopp shouted out, "Fire drill's over. Get back in a line."

I had never been happier to hear his voice. I was seconds away from throwing up all over the anthill. I wondered if the queen realized how lucky she had been.

"Madam Queen, the giants have taken the war against us to another level. They are now spewing some type of disgusting liquid throughout the land. Within the watery substance are scrambled eggs and turkey sausage. Half of our army is drowning as we speak."

The rest of the day was business as usual and nothing worth reporting, except maybe when word got around that one of the kindergartners had taken an entire jar of glue to the bathroom and somehow had glued toilet paper to all the walls. Kindergarteners are awesome. I wish I owned a pair.

That night for dinner was chili. My mom makes the world's best chili. No joke, she has even won several chili cook-offs. The rest of her food is barely edible enough for a dog, but when it comes to chili she has a special talent. I think it all comes from the bay leaves.

According to her bay leaves are an exotic plant

that grows only on the west side of the highest mountain in Peru. To get these leaves a local villager has to climb the mountain, risking life and limb. The mountain is also infested with cougars who dine on the flesh of men like frogs eat flies. To harvest these bay leaves one must survive the cougars and the climb and then snowboard down the west side of the mountain. I don't believe a word of this story because I asked Isaac's grandpa if it snowed in Peru, and he said it can snow on the highest mountaintops in the Peru mountains called the Andes, but when I asked him if Peru villagers snowboarded he looked at me like I had worms coming out of my ears.

My guess is she buys them at the grocery store when she is done with her Mom meetings and they come from some factory in Mexico. Either way, the bay leaves do add a very special element for me. I get to hunt for them in the chili. You see, my mom says these bay leaves are highly poisonous if consumed in their entirety and only the flavor of the leaf is good. So she gives me a big spoon, and I take it and stir it around the chili hunting for the leaves. She always puts four of them in the chili. The first three are usually easy to find, but the fourth is as sneaky as a ninja in a bamboo forest.

On this particular night I found the first two right away and then freaked out as my hunting located something much worse than a bay leaf. A worm. Todd was eating dinner with his friends at some pizza place at the mall, and I guess before leaving he thought he would make his mark on our dinner. Needless to say I pretended that I started feeling sick and only ate crackers that night. Stupid Todd. But if I thought that was bad, it was nothing compared to what happened the next day at school. I have forever deemed it The Day of the Great Switcheroo.

CHAPTER 2

It all started innocently enough, a little geography lesson about the Great Plains and some science in which we learned that Isaac Newton let an apple hit him on the head and it lead to one of the greatest scientific discoveries of mankind. Brian teased Isaac about how we should all get apples and throw them at him so he could be famous. Brian wasn't being mean, he was just having fun, and Isaac just laughed. In fact it was that kind of day, a lot of kidding around and laughter, and then Mr. Hopp announced the Great Switcheroo.

"Class, as most of you with older siblings know we have done the same two plays in alternating years for as long as I can remember. One year we do *Beauty and the Beast* and then the next year we do *Robin Hood* and then back to *Beauty and the Beast* and so on and so forth." Mr. Hopp had our attention. Something was going on. I wasn't sure what it was, but something in my gut was telling me it was going to be bad. I would never claim to have the gift of seeing into the future, but every now and then I get a little sick feeling inside my belly right before something bad happens, and I was getting that sick feeling right then and there.

"These are two timeless plays, and it doesn't hurt that the school has already paid for all the props associated with them. Yet, I am torn. I look at this class and see the super star talent that exists. Tiffany alone could headline an off-Broadway show right now." Tiffany beamed. Within the fluorescent lights that engulf a classroom sometimes it is hard to make out exact facial features of an individual person, but in this case I could *actually see* Tiffany's head get bigger. It swelled almost twice its normal size. I hoped it would pop like a giant tick.

Mr. Hopp continued, "It seems unfair to pass along to you the same script that we've used time and time again. I know some of you even have older siblings who have been in these plays before, like Hank whose older brother Todd played a fine Merry Man. Hank, tell the class how do you feel about putting on the same play your brother has already done?"

All heads swiveled to me as if I was a giant magnet. Caught completely off guard I said the first thing that came to my mouth and played perfectly into Mr. Hopp's diabolical plan. He used me like a pawn that day. I haven't built a time machine yet, but when I do there are a few days that I intend to go back and visit immediately. The Day of the Great Switcheroo is most certainly one of them. Until then I will have to live with the fact that when Mr. Hopp asked me how I felt about doing the same play as my horrible older brother I said, "I don't like it at all, Mr. Hopp. Not at all."

Mr. Hopp almost jumped up to the ceiling as he responded to what I had said with an emphatic, "Exactly! And frankly, Hank, you shouldn't have to." He stopped for dramatic effect. It worked. We all stared at him. You could almost hear the gears in each of our brains as we searched for the answer to the question that we were all left with: What in the world was Mr. Hopp up to? He let us hang there for about three minutes, which I have to admit doesn't sound like much time and maybe you are sitting there saying, three minutes? That's nothing. Well, next time Christmas morning comes and you are standing in front of your biggest present I want you to wait preciously three minutes before opening it. That's right! Three minutes now seems like a very long time, doesn't it?

After the wait of a century he finally said it, "Class, let's redo *Robin Hood.*"

No one said anything.

"From the first telling of *Robin Hood* in some remote village in Europe people have been led to believe how Robin Hood stole from the rich and gave to the poor. Of how he saved the land and the beautiful Maid Marion." Tiffany Green's head got even bigger. It now looked like a giant balloon. I wished I had a needle. "We've been told of how he won every battle with the Sheriff of Nottingham, but what if we changed that? What if we *rewrote* the story so that when Robin Hood goes to fight the Sheriff . . . the Sheriff wins!"

Yes, I almost screamed out loud. For the past few

days Isaac had constantly reminded me of how he would stick a sword through my heart and vanquish me. All in good fun of course, but how sweet it would be to turn the tables and get to defeat him! I looked toward Isaac in the front and saw him sag into his seat. The weight of his fall into sudden death was too much for him. I would be the hero, the winner, the champion, the—and then it hit me. Like a ton of bricks. Like a freight train carrying a ton of bricks. Like two freight trains carrying a factory that makes tons of bricks. And even before Mr. Hopp said the words I knew what was going to come out of his mouth.

"The Sheriff will beat Robin Hood and as the crowd sits in shock and awe, our new hero, the Sheriff of Nottingham will turn toward the beautiful Maid Marian and kiss her!"

I heard Tiffany Green let out a little mouse squeak, and she clapped her hands wildly together. This couldn't be happening. I had to stop it somehow. I thought quickly and raised my hand.

"Mr. Hopp, Robin Hood is a literary classic. I mean the story of Robin Hood has stood the test of time. I don't think we should go messing with it."

Tiffany countered with, "Mr. Hopp, I have to politely disagree with Hank. The world is ready for a new version of *Robin Hood*. I think your idea is fantastic and will keep the audience on their toes."

Mr. Hopp said, "I couldn't agree more Tiffany. Let's do it!"

Whatever happened the rest of the day I have no memory of it. It was like a black hole had expanded over earth and everything that was good and fair was sucked deep into the recesses of the blackness never to be seen from again.

I woke up the next day and didn't have a

recollection of how I had made my way to my bed that night. There was no worm lying next to me, but honestly I wouldn't have cared if there had been. The world had ended. Tyranny and evil had won. I would have to kiss Tiffany Green. Somewhere I realized it was the weekend, and I wouldn't have to go back to school till Monday. Then an idea started forming. Maybe some way I could escape *ever* having to go to school again. Now I know every kid that has ever walked the surface of this planet has had this same thought and there have been many attempts to never have to go back. If you haven't heard of the top three school escape attempts here they are:

1) David Pearson, Providence Rhode Island. David, or Davey as he was called by his closest friends, attempted a classic ditch school method. He went for the sick day, but Davey had eyes on the biggest prize, to never go back to

school again. He decided if he could convince his mom and dad that he had some type of rare and infectious disease he would be safe from school forever. He took a magic marker and painted bright purple spots all over his skin. Now that move had been done by almost every kid. How Davey took it to another level was he built a website about the Purple Dot Disease. So when he was discovered with the purple dots and faked being sick so well that his parents thought he might actually be sick, they went to their computers and looked up what purple dots meant. From there they landed on Davey's own website—of course they had no clue he had built it. They freaked out and for five seconds Davey thought he was on his way. That was until he heard talk of going to the emergency room.

Davey quickly aborted his plan because he had an intense fear of hospitals.

2) Bryce McCallugh, San Diego, California. Bryce will forever be nicknamed The Skid Kid after his attempt. Bryce appealed to what is labeled "the mom gross-out factor." By three years old every boy learns that grossing out mom is not only fun, but can also prove very beneficial when wanting to get out of chores or in Bryce's case, school. Bryce purchased ten chocolate bars at the local gas station and then he took every pair of white underwear he owned. Every single pair and he melted the chocolate bars right down the middle. This created what is known as the brown streak or brown skid effect. It makes it look like you have poo stained your underwear. Now no mom can handle the brown streak. It takes a

mom's gross out meter and maxes it out. Bryce figured that there was no way his mom would let him wear those streak filled underroos, and no way would she ever put him on the school bus without underwear. His plan almost worked—if it hadn't been for his older brother Marcus. Marcus heard his mom scream about the streaks and went to tease his brother for streaking his underwear when he saw the ten wrappers in the garbage can. He immediately snitched out Bryce who not only had to go to school, but also got grounded for the entire month. Older brothers are the worst.

3) Kelly Hicks, Mankato, Minnesota.

Kelly came the closest of all the escape attempts. She orchestrated a complex system dubbed the Father Forge. She was able to get her dad to sign a note for her to miss after school gymnastic practice one day, but instead of giving the note to her teacher she kept it and went ahead and did the gymnastics practice. Kelly had a much longer-term goal in mind than missing one practice. What she did was take the note to her bedroom and for the next six weeks she carefully copied her father's signature over and over again. Soon, she could sign her dad's name perfectly and only a handwriting expert employed by the government would be able to tell the difference. She then wrote a note excusing her from class the rest of the year and went to turn it in to her teacher. It was the perfect plan with the perfect signature. Her only mistake was spelling. In her haste to create the note she had misspelled the day of the week she was turning the note in on. She had written Wendesday instead of Wednesday. It was a simple mistake, but a costly one. Kelly was grounded for over three months and lost all phone privileges (which to a girl is the worst of all punishments). Her dad had to create an entirely new signature so that Kelly wouldn't be able to forge again.

I spent all Saturday morning drawing out possible escape plans, strategies, and concepts. Four hours of hard work and about 60 sheets of paper later it was almost lunchtime when I threw my hands in the air and gave up. I had thought of different pretend illnesses, making fake throw-up, heating up the thermometer, but I knew it had all been done and failed. I had nothing. It was hopeless. I would have to kiss Tiffany Green.

"NOOOOOOO!" I shouted. From downstairs I heard Todd shout back, "Shut up, Worm!"

I sat there thinking of how horrible my older brother was and how he deserved to be shot out of a canon into an immense lake of slime with piranhas and sharks in it when I felt a hand on my shoulder.

At first I figured it was Todd about to inflict some kind of torture on me, but when I turned around it was Sue's hand. Isaac stood next to her. Sue spoke first, "I'm so sorry, Hank."

"Yeah, man." Isaac said. "Part of me is like super relieved not to have to kiss her myself, but I know it's going to be worse. She has wanted to kiss you since the first grade."

He was wrong. She has wanted to kiss me since kindergarten. At naptime she would put her cot right next to mine and stare at me while we were going to sleep. At finger paint time she would make hearts and write my name inside. One time at recess she and her friends all ganged up on me and tried to get me to play house in which I was the dad, she was the mom, and all the other kids were our children.

Sue and Isaac were both in other kindergarten classes that year so they weren't aware just how bad it was. Tiffany Green had more than a crush on me. It was some type of fatal attraction, and I swear she must sit up at night to this very day writing my initials and hers in little heart balloons in some pink journal. I saw one balloon like that carved into the wooden playground equipment. At first I thought, who would put the word *HAT* in a heart balloon, and then Isaac pointed it out. Hank And Tiffany. HAT. Ugh.

We decided to get out of my house and Sue and Isaac did their best to take my mind off of the kiss, but nothing worked.

Sue threw in the towel, which is what a boxer

does when they decide they can't keep fighting. "I'm done, Hank. I know it stinks, but you have to snap out of it. It's one kiss."

Isaac and I both looked at her and at the exact same time said, "With Tiffany Green."

"I know. I just want to not let it ruin the rest of our lives. We need advice on how to handle this."

Isaac lit up. "Let's ask my grandpa."

It was a fantastic idea. Within a short bike ride we were in Isaac's house talking to his grandpa Roger. Roger was sitting in an oversized chair that he called a recliner. I don't know why old people insist in sitting in these things. We watched Roger struggle to get up from the chair for about twenty minutes, and when he finally had escaped from the chair it took Isaac's grandpa a solid ten minutes to get his breath back and recover.

Once he finally was able to talk we told him about

our current predicament and how I would rather die than kiss Tiffany Green. He sat quietly listening, and after we were finished he told Isaac to grab some ginger snaps from the pantry. Isaac's grandpa loved ginger snaps the way that kids love a swimming pool.

"I do my best thinking with a ginger snap in hand," Roger said and ate two cookies.

He offered us some as well which we gladly accepted. The sound of us all munching into the ginger snaps made me think of a robot factory. Snap, munch, crumble. I really don't even like ginger snaps that much, but I enjoy the sound they make when you eat them, especially with friends.

"Say, Worm, did you know that a potato makes electricity, like a battery?"

I shook my head no all the while wondering what in the world potatoes had to do with kissing Tiffany

Green. Maybe the ray gun I believe he has hidden in the house somewhere runs off of potatoes, and he was going to let me use it to zap Tiffany, but I doubted it. Adults usually don't think violence is the best way to solve problems.

"Well, it's true. The juice inside a potato contains a lot of chemicals, and you can actually cause a chemical reaction by inserting just the right type of metals into the potato. I have actually seen someone connect a bunch of potatoes and use the electricity they made to light up a flashlight."

Again I had no clue what any of this had to do with my problem, but it was fascinating anyway. Not for the last time I thought how cool it was that Isaac's grandpa was a retired astronaut.

"I learned that from a girl named Susan Collier. She was in the astronaut training program with me and a few other guys. She was a pain in the behind. None of us liked her at all. One day at training they put us into pairs and wouldn't you know it, I got stuck with Susan. Then they gave us a small backpack and took us out to the middle of the desert and told us, 'Find your way home.' Then they left in a Jeep, and I was stuck there in the middle of the hot desert with Susan Collier and in the bag was nothing but a few pieces of wire, potatoes, one bottle of water, a light bulb, and some other odds and ends— none of which seemed helpful for surviving in the desert let alone making our way back to the base. I wasn't happy to say the least."

"What did you do, Grandpa?" Isaac asked.

"Nothing, Isaac. I did nothing. Susan did it all. She took the backpack and within seconds had made a water filtration system that you could stick into a cactus and get juice from, and at night she used those potatoes to make a flashlight, and we navigated our way back to base. I still didn't like Susan, but I had admiration for her, and I learned an important lesson that day in the desert."

Sue piped in, "Was it that even people you don't like can be helpful?"

Roger snapped his fingers, "Roger that, Sue. Also, I learned that the show must go on. It didn't matter who I got paired with on that assignment. What mattered was completing the mission."

I knew exactly what Isaac's grandpa was getting at. The show must go on. A man has to do what a man has to do. I was the Sheriff of Nottingham, and if I was supposed to defeat Robin Hood and kiss Maid Marian then by golly, I was going to be the best Sheriff of Nottingham the world had ever seen!

I just had to suck it up. That week at school play rehearsal was a breeze. I never had to kiss Tiffany Green in rehearsals. Mr. Hopp wanted to save that first kiss for the stage, although Tiffany did her best to convince him we should practice it.

Instead we had plenty of sword fighting and pretend dying. In Scene Three, Brian as Prince John had the best death ever. He would scream loudly and fall to the ground flopping like a fish, screaming, "Revenge! Revenge!" It was great.

The night of the play I went in thinking I was going to be a hero and remembered what Roger had said: What mattered was completing the mission. As the curtain lifted I walked out ready to give a performance of a lifetime.

CHAPTER 3

Mr. Hopp's version of *Robin Hood* began with Prince John (Brian) and The Sheriff of Nottingham (me) talking about how much we love money and how we are going to tax the poor to build a castle made of gold. The opening line comes from the Sheriff and he is supposed to say, "Hello, your majesty. I have just come back from taxing some poor people." And then I hand him a bag of gold.

I had this line down. I had practiced it about 100 times. Brian and I had this great idea for me to throw the money bag to him, and he would catch it behind his back. We had done this like 200 times and were successful more often than not. I was ready. I was prepared.

I was wrong.

I totally freaked out.

I had walked three steps onto the stage when I was hit with the worst case of stage fright in the entire universe. As I walked out to Brian I was fine, but then when I turned and saw the crowd watching something happened. It was like my brain went into a deep freeze.

First I stopped walking and just froze up. I was staring at them while they were staring at me. I couldn't move a single muscle. Then I started sweating. Sue watched from behind the scenes, dressed in her Merry Men outfit, and said it looked like someone had just drenched me with a water balloon.

Then I can recall Brian shouting my name. "Sheriff. Sheriff. *Hank!* Is that bag my gold you just got from the poor people?"

He was trying to save me. And it helped. Kinda. I

could move again, which was progress. I turned toward him, but my mouth was broken. I couldn't formulate words. I tried, but my mouth just moved up and down and the only sound that came out was like a ghost being hit by a bus. It was like, "Boooaaahhhugg" or something like that.

Brian looked at me like I was from Planet Xtremous or something. He said, "Well, Sheriff why don't you throw me that bag of gold so I can begin building my golden castle?"

I looked down at the bag in my hand. I had completely forgotten it was there. I looked back at him. Back at the bag. It wasn't really gold in the bag, it was full of wadded up paper and one brick. The paper made it look full of money and the brick made it heavy enough for the audience to think it might actually be gold. I looked back at Brian and went to throw the bag to him, but it never made it to him.

Instead I threw it way too high and it hit the lights above the stage. Then the lights broke off and swung into the fake wooden trees that were painted at the back of the stage designed to make the audience believe we were actually in medieval times. One light hit a tree dead on, knocking it over. The other light landed at the bottom of the tree and burst into flames. I was pushed from behind as Mr. Hopp ran out with a fire extinguisher and started putting the fire out.

His push made me turn back toward the audience. I could see Todd laughing hysterically next to my mom. Farther down in the same row was Mrs. Wallace the Walrus who was smiling as well. It was the first and last time I ever saw her smile.

Suddenly I had this weird, tangy taste in the back of my throat. I felt like I was going to throw up. The people in the front row saw my face turn green and watched me grab for my stomach.

Everyone knows that when a kid grabs for his stomach there is about a 35% chance they are going to hurl. The people in front got up quickly and ran out of the way, but I didn't hurl. Instead I said my first lines, "Hello, your majesty. I have just come back from taxing some poor people."

Then I started walking forward. I have no clue why. I think back to this day and still cannot account for any of my actions, but I was walking forward and even held up my hand like the bag of gold was still clasped tightly in my fist, but it wasn't. There was nothing there, and I was not walking toward Brian. Instead I was walking right toward the end of the stage, which had about an eight-foot dropoff until you hit the first row. I just walked and walked. I could hear people shouting

"Stop!" but I never did.

I walked right off the stage and landed on the ground, belly first. Isaac says you could hear the sound of me landing over everything else that was going on and that Mr. Hopp dropped the fire extinguisher and came running to me, the fire still burning. By now it had also caught hold of the painted wooden castle backdrop.

Mr. Hopp came rushing to my side and carried me back up the steps. I think his plan was to get me backstage and make sure I was okay when he caught sight of the now raging fire. He dropped me to the ground and went running toward the fire. I stood up. I was okay, just your standard eight-foot belly flop, nothing a kid can't handle. I looked out toward the crowd.

They were all out of their chairs, most heading toward the doors when suddenly it started raining, except it wasn't really rain. It was the sprinkler system that is designed to go off in the event of a fire.

Just then from my left I heard Tiffany Green's voice. "You're not ruining this play for me, Hank. Pucker up." And before I even registered what she was saying her slimy lips touched mine. She held the kiss for what seemed like an eternity, the whole time making that smooching noise. She had taken her arms and wrapped them around me so even as I squirmed to get loose I couldn't. I had no idea Tiffany Green was that strong!

And then I blacked out.

In the end everything was okay. No one had gotten hurt and the only damage was to one set of lights and the Robin Hood set. At class I was a living legend. Tales of the fire and the Great Freeze are told to this very day. Mr. Hopp never mentioned it. EVER. I think in his mind he pretends none of it ever happened. I am still haunted by the memory of the play, of how we spent an entire week planning out *Robin Hood*, the costumes everyone made and never got to act in, but apparently I'm the only one. Everyone else looks back and just laughs, but I haven't gotten there yet.

Every time I try to think of how funny it really was The Kiss comes to mind. I believe that Tiffany Green was wearing some type of blueberry lip gunk because for weeks after the play the smell of blueberries made me want to hurl. To this day I don't eat blueberry flavored anything.

A month after the play Isaac, Sue, and I found another HAT heart carved into a tree at Sawyer Park and this one had little lips puckered up into a kiss all around it. We spent practically all day carving over it. Todd was the worst of them all, he dressed a worm up as Robin Hood complete with a bow and everything and hid it in my shoe one day. Two days after that he had drawn a picture of two worms kissing and put it on the fridge. Mom took it down and told him to stop, but I know better. Todd will never stop. Older brothers are like the worst disease ever—except for girls who want to kiss you.

MY NEW NEIGHBOR THE WEREWOLF

It was nearly the end of summer. Less than four weeks to go. My Super Friends and I were taking advantage of every day left. Earlier in the week I had gotten my mom to pick up a bunch of our friends for an awesome game of kickball. I hit two homeruns and Sue had made a catch from outfield that made all of our jaws drop.

Brian Ekerson hit a big shot out to left field that was surely a triple if not a home run, and it looked like it was going to go way over Sue's head. Bryan had already started the classic kid home run trot.

The home run trot or better known by its acronym HRT comes in a variety of looks. There's the

Slow Trot with the loud base stomp as the face looks forward as if in focus. This is a style often chosen by the more humble who like to act like it was no big deal, just a home run anyone could have done it.

Then there's the galloping trot with big long strides, small head nods to the baseman as the homerun kicker makes his rounds. Brian went for the galloping trot, but mixed in some crowd pleasers with finger points to the kids watching. Now don't get me wrong, I'm a huge fan of the galloping trot, but I could have done without the crowd pleasers.

In this particular case Brian was really layering it on. He had gone with the classic finger pointing like it's a gun move, and as he rounded first he "shot" at the baseman there.

Unfortunately for Brian Sue hadn't given up on the play and she had bolted like lightning to deep outfield then jumping like some wild gazelle she just made contact with the ball and forced into a high bounce, but at the same time stopping its forward trajectory. As she fell to the ground the ball began its descent, and she reached up and grasped it. Pure kickball genius.

Then yesterday we had taken out water guns, and Sue's dad had put red food coloring in the water so when you got shot it looked like blood. It was sweet . . . and pretty tasty if I do say so myself.

And today marked three weeks two days until the start of the school year. We needed to do something. To let just one day get by this close to the end would be a travesty. We sat in a circle on my front lawn. Isaac was throwing out ideas for the day and the lead idea was seeing if we could get my mom to drive us to see the new movie that had opened up the weekend before. It was an action movie, *Thermal Thunder,* in which the good guy was a Navy Seal trying to capture an enemy submarine before it got close enough to America to shoot its nuclear missiles. It sounded cool. Besides there was a pop-a-shot game at the movie theater, and last time we were there I set the high score, and I wanted to see if my record still stood.

I was just about to get up and go ask mom when we heard a large truck come rolling down the street. It was bright green. I mean like *bright fluorescent* green and on the side written in yellow was GREENE & GREENE MOVING COMPANY.

Sue said it first. "The new neighbors are here!"

About a year ago Mrs. Henderson had moved from the corner house down the street. She told us she was going to move to Mobile, Alabama, to be closer to her son. She was originally from that area and had this really cool "Southern" way of saying things. Like when she told us to have a good summer she said, "Y'all have a gawd summa." We missed her because she would make lemonade for us, and she paid Isaac ten dollars to mow her lawn. That was good money in our world, and we were short a lot of candy this summer as a result of that income being gone. I guess the recession hits everyone.

None of us knew who was moving in. All we knew was that a SOLD sign had been placed in front of Mrs. Henderson's old house. There had been lots of neighborhood wondering as to who was coming, but it was all pure guessing. We just hoped they had a kid our age, and we *really* hoped they didn't have a kid Todd's age. The last thing the neighborhood needed was another Todd.

The truck stopped, and two guys in screaming green uniforms jumped out and moved to the back. They lifted up the rear door of the truck. It was totally dark, and you couldn't see a thing. Then they pulled a ramp out from under the truck and disappeared into the darkness inside.

They were gone a few minutes, and Sue, Isaac, and I were just about to start walking closer to see if we could get a look inside the truck when out of the darkness a huge black bear appeared. It was standing tall on its back legs, the bear's mouth was open wide as if in mid-roar, and razor sharp teeth the size of my head spiked out of the bear's mouth. Its paws were raised as if about to swipe down at some poor kid with humongous claws longer than my arms. It moved down the ramp . . . fast. Sue, Isaac, and I started walking backward. If one of us had turned to run the rest would have instantly followed.

Then we noticed the moving guys behind the bear and realized it wasn't actually alive. This monster was dead and stuffed. We watched the movers wheel the bear into the house and then they came back and a large wolf followed, then a coyote, a large bird that Isaac said was a Red Tailed Hawk. Next was a deer head, then a lion's head. It took the movers about two hours to get all the animals out. We counted 23 animals overall. Isaac guessed our new neighbor was a hunter.

"I bet a taxidermist," said a voice behind us. It was Todd. Not only could I tell by the voice, but the stench of his breath was unmistakable. We all turned and couldn't believe we had allowed him to sneak up behind us. We jumped back ready to run.

"Shut up, Worm. If I was going to mess with you I already would have. What all did you losers see?"

Out of fear of what would happen if we didn't reply we told him about the bear, and he nodded his head and said, "Cool." Then he turned around and left.

Once he was out of sight Sue shouted at me, "I

thought you said he was at a friend's house!"

"He was. He must have gotten back while we were staring at the truck."

Isaac wiped his brow. "Man, we just got lucky. He could have done anything to us. Why don't you think he messed with us?"

I shook my head. I had no clue. Todd lives to torment us and opportunities to catch us unaware are few. He ordinarily should have attacked us. I felt like someone must feel when a giant tornado passes feet from their house and doesn't do any damage.

We stood in silence for a moment and then turned back to the truck. Sue asked, "What's a taxidermist?"

Isaac and I had no clue. I threw out a guess, "Maybe someone who does taxes for dermatologists . . . you know the doctors who mess with people's skin. Todd had to go to one when he got bad zits."

"Gross," said Sue and Isaac in unison.

"I still say he's a hunter," Isaac said, our attention back at the truck. "Yep. Hunter for sure. Probably goes on safaris and expeditions."

We all nodded our heads.

Another big GREENE & GREENE truck appeared later that day, but we didn't see any more animals get unloaded. Just the usual stuff like boxes and furniture. The owner never arrived that day and we went home when it got dark.

At dinner mom ordered pizza and she asked if we had seen the new neighbor arrive. Todd and I both said no and then Todd told her about seeing all the animals getting unloaded.

"Sounds like a taxidermist," Mom said.

"That's what I told Worm and his friends,"

replied Todd. Mom shook her head. For years she had corrected my older brother every time he called me Worm, but she had finally given up. Now when he used that horrible name she just shook her head.

Adults can always be counted on for two things. One, they will always insist you make your bed even though everyone knows you will just mess it up all over again the very next night. And two, they give up easily. In certain kid circles this phenomenon is referred to as "The Wear Down." For example every kid knows that if you ask often enough for a certain present you will eventually get it. If you do a chore badly enough for long enough they will in time stop asking you to do it. And if you referrer to your younger brother as a worm they will one day stop correcting you. If kids gave up as quickly as adults do, nothing would ever get done.

"What's a taxidermist?" I asked my mom.

"Someone who takes dead animals and stuffs them," she said.

Then Todd chimed in. "Yeah. A taxidermist waits till very late at night. Right when an animal . . . or person . . . is sleeping and then he sneaks up on them and gets right next to their ear."

Todd had gotten out of his chair and was walking closer to me. Closer. Closer. Until he was mere inches from my ear and then he talked low, just above a whisper, "And as the animal begins to sense that something is close, a taxidermist reaches into his pocket and pulls out a special whistle. A very special whistle that makes a sound like a wolf howling in the night and if the whistle is blown close enough the sound will reach into the heart of the animal and stop it from beating. The animal will die right on the spot."

Todd moved quickly to my other ear. Now he

whispered so low I had to strain myself to hear him. "Then the taxidermist quickly takes the now dead animal to his basement where he keeps tools that only a taxidermist has. Large knives, sharper than swords. An apron so that the blood won't-"

"That's enough, Todd. Your brother is just messing with you, Hank. You just bought yourself dishes tonight, Todd."

I stuck my tongue out at him. Mom saw me and said, "And with that move young man you just bought yourself trash duty. Roll the trashcan out to the street. Then I want you both to brush your teeth and get ready for bed."

Todd reached under the table and pinched my leg hard. I screamed. My mom, of course, didn't see Todd pinch me and thought I was screaming at having to take the trash out. "Well now, Hank, if that is your attitude you can do the dishes AND take out the trash."

Todd smiled at me and quickly left the room before I could explain to my mom what had happened. Todd. Ugh.

I took the dishes into the kitchen and started putting them into the dishwasher. My only consolation was that it had been pizza delivery night so there weren't any pots or pans to do. I went to the garage and began rolling the trashcan down the driveway. It was heavier than a backpack full of math books and I figured Todd had taken the time to put bricks in it just to make it harder for me. I was halfway down the driveway, mumbling under my breath how I wished I was an only child, when suddenly I realized how quiet it was outside, as if every animal had left town on vacation.

I looked around and saw that a fog had rolled into the night and if not for the lampposts that lined the street

I wouldn't have been able to see anything. I could just make out Sue's house across the street, and as I made my way to the end of the driveway I looked down to see if I would be able to see Isaac's house, but it was lost in the fog. As I peered down the road I suddenly heard a car door close.

I squinted my eyes really tightly and could make out a dark red car a little ways down parked in front of Mrs. Henderson's old house. I could just barely see the shadow of some large figure. It was walking toward her house and then it suddenly stopped and began to turn. I don't know why, but I had the irresistible urge to hide. I ducked behind the trashcan and leaned out, just enough so I could see the shadow figure. I stood still as an oak tree. I knew that whoever or whatever was out there was listening for me.

CHAPTER 2

I held my hands over my mouth and took a deep breath

in and held it. The figure stood silent and then turned

back and started walking away. Soon it disappeared into

the fog and was gone. I waited wondering if it would

reemerge when suddenly my mom's voice broke the eerie

silence of the night.

"Hank! Get finished with that trashcan and get

inside."

No! I turned into the fog hoping above all hope

that the . . . thing in the fog hadn't heard my name, but I

knew better. I couldn't see it, but I knew without a

shadow of a doubt that it lurked there still, deep in the

fog, and my mom had given me away. I ran inside thanking my mom for what no doubt would prove to be the end of my life. She ushered me up the stairs and into my room. I thought I wouldn't sleep a wink that night, but like most kids I was asleep almost instantly.

At 3:47 that night I was awaken from my deep slumber. I only knew the time because my Superman alarm clock displayed it brightly in the darkness of my room. I heard a loud crash from outside and ran to my window. My trashcan had been knocked down and trash spilled all over the street.

"Payback for watching," I whispered to myself. I watched the garbage can for what seemed like an eternity and nothing more happened. I eventually crawled back to bed and fell asleep.

The next day I woke up to Isaac and Sue knocking on the door. I opened the door, and they both were ecstatic and full of energy. Isaac was basically jumping up and down in place, and Sue was waving her arms saying, "You have to look at your trash. Something has been eating it!"

My eyes grew ten times their normal size. "Did you say . . . *eating?*"

"Yes! All the bags are ripped opened and whatever did it must have had decent sized claws because you can actually see where it tore the bags open."

Isaac said, "Yeah, it is so cool! It's like some type of huge animal got at your leftovers!"

"Guys, I have to tell you what I saw last night."

"Later. Hurry up, come on!" And Sue and Isaac grabbed me by the arms and started leading me down to the garbage can. I dug my heels into the ground and turned on them.

"No. Wait! You *have* to hear this."

They both stopped and looked at me. Super Friends know exactly when it's time to talk and exactly when it's time to listen. Isaac and Sue knew this was a listen time. "Sue. Isaac. Last night I think I saw a monster." And then I told them the rest of my story.

When I finished I expected both of them to say something like, "Wow. That is crazy! A monster in our neighborhood." Or "It was a vampire! We have to get some stakes or garlic powder." Maybe even, "It knows your name. We have to move to another country where you will be safe from it, like China, and we can sell all of our things and become rice farmers and live out the rest of our days pretending wea noa speaka da Englisha."

Instead all I got was Sue asking me, "Are you sure it wasn't just a man?"

Then Isaac jumped in with, "Yeah, maybe it was just the new neighbor. Look, there's a red car parked in front of Mrs. Henderson's house right now."

I turned my head and looked down the road and sure enough there it was. The red car I had seen in the fog. I nodded my head a little, my brain in overdrive trying to put this piece of information with what I had seen in the fog last night combined with the new knowledge that something had been eating my trash. The truth jumped out at me like a snake in the grass. It was so obvious. I hit myself in the head for not seeing it right away.

"He's a werewolf."

Isaac and Sue, who only mere seconds ago had been ignoring me jumped in. There's was no denying the evidence that literally laid before us smelling up the street like a hobo who had eaten a bad can of beans.

"A werewolf," said Isaac. "Right here in our own neighborhood. What should we do?"

"We'll have to do some investigating." And Sue smiled as big as Sue can smile.

Investigating may be one of the coolest things in the realm of mankind. I have never actually looked up the definition of investigating, but I bet it is something like this <u>Investigating:</u> To look for clues by sneaking, snooping, and hiding. To become a spy and do espionage as you discover the truth that lies beneath the surface. To collect information like a detective.

In the last attempt of the Super Friends to be spies we found out we were really good at it. You see, Sue and her dad had just finished a cool book about a spy from London who had saved the queen from an assassination attempt, so she had decided we should play spies that day.

Isaac's grandpa had three old trench coats he let us borrow, which were so cool; when we put them on we looked just like world-class spies. We didn't really have any plans on who or what we should spy on when suddenly we heard Todd yell out, "Worm! You look so stupid. What did you do steal some old guy's clothes?"

Then he started laughing that hideous Todd laugh and joining him in laughing was none other than Todd's friend Gus Henry. Gus was a weasel. He was super skinny and tall with red hair that was so bright I swear it glowed at night. He had red freckles that covered his skin and little beady green eyes. I had never met Gus's parents, but if one of them wasn't a weasel then he must be adopted.

After the two of them laughed at us they went into my backyard. That's when we decided to spy on them. It was extremely dangerous, but everyone knows that danger is a spy's middle name so we weren't scared. Or if we were we didn't tell each other.

We had hid in the bushes watching them and listening, which if you don't know is a big part of what spies do. We discovered all kinds of interesting classified information. We wrote it down in a spiral notebook that Sue had named *Our Spy Book*. (I know, it wasn't a very good name, but we couldn't exactly tell Sue that). Here is some of the information we discovered that afternoon:

- Gus failed math and had to take summer school to make it up, a fact he was trying to keep from his parents. (Instantly we knew we could sell this information to Gus's weasel parents for at least five dollars.)

- Todd had hidden dirt in the cupcakes my mom had made for Sue, Isaac, and me. (This was great information because we hadn't had any yet and managed to stay away from the cupcakes telling my mom we had decided to go on a diet.

This ensured we kept the number of times I had involuntarily eaten dirt to 38.)

- Todd thought Becky Novak was cute. (Once we learned this, we decided to quit playing spies for the day. No one wants to know who in the world Todd finds cute. I know that I hope this girl moves far away, maybe even becomes a rice farmer so that she never has to face the embarrassment of Todd asking her to a dance.)

When Sue decided we should do some investigating we made our way over to the Secret Hideout. We did the usual ritual of entering with Sue holding the rope that opened the latch to the gate, me listening for Isaac, and Isaac barking like a dog seven times. He hadn't made it back to the gate in the five seconds from when we open it, so he had to say the password to get in. *Jumping Beans In My Pants.*

We climbed up the rope to the Secret Hideout and even though there was massive temptation to do a backflip off the plank onto the trampoline we went straight in and began devising a plan to investigate if the new neighbor was truly a werewolf.

Sue started the conversation by listing the known facts of a werewolf. I am sure you are very aware of these, and I won't go into detail. It was a list of the usual stuff, you know, full moon turns into a werewolf and eats people, has extra-hairy arms and legs, loves to eats people's trash—stuff like that.

Once we made it through the list of stuff we had to look for, it was time to begin deciding how we should conduct our investigation.

Isaac said, "I think we should start with basic observation techniques. We should hide out and watch

Mrs. Henderson's house."

Sue said, "Great idea. I think we should do it stakeout style." I loved it! Stakeout style means doing the spying at night as if you were a cop on a stakeout of the bad guys. Sue kept going, "My dad has walkie talkies he sometimes uses for work. I'll grab them, and we can use them tonight. The biggest problem is there are only two."

"No problem at all," I said. "Isaac, you and Sue will each have one, and I will just listen in through one of those." I learned a long time ago with Isaac and Sue that since they were only children they weren't as good at sharing as I am and to stop a lot of potential conflicts I always throw out me sharing while they have their own as much as possible. Selfish only gets you so far in life. Besides, it always resulted in one of them saying they owed me and everyone knows when someone owes you they practically have to give in to the next favor you ask.

Someday I'll cash in those favors they owe me, maybe when I need a new kidney or something, and they won't be able to say no.

"I owe you," Isaac said. (See what I mean!)

Sue chimed in, "Okay, that's settled. So I say we begin the stakeout when the sun goes down. You guys need to ask to stay the night here. We'll use the Secret Hideout as a base. I'll tell my dad we're doing a sleepover up here again tonight. Shouldn't be a problem."

We both said cool and then we all went home to get permission. We went to my house first, and my mom was quick to say yes, but told me I had to pick up the trash that was in the street from the knocked over trashcan. She blamed me saying I hadn't put it out right. I wanted to say that she should blame the werewolf that moved in down the street, but thought maybe not.

Next we rode our bikes down to Isaac's house.

Roger was inside cooking over a large pot of something. At first I thought it might be space spaghetti, but quickly realized by the smell that it wasn't. In fact it smelled horrible.

"What are you cooking, Roger?" I asked.

"Glad you asked, Worm. I'm not actually cooking anything. Isaac, we have fruit flies." And just as he said that I noticed four little flies buzz by my face. I swatted at them, but they were too fast, and I missed by a mile.

Roger saw me miss and smiled. "Don't feel bad, Worm. I've been trying all day to swat those suckers and I've missed every time. It's like they're the red baron and maneuver right out of harm's way at the last second. Crafty little devils, but I found the solution. A little bit of vinegar and boiling water. Supposed to cure the pest right away. Also read about using red wine and leaving it out in half empty glasses, but didn't want to support underage fly drinking." And Roger laughed and laughed.

Isaac, Sue, and I all just looked at each other, no clue what he thought was so funny. Old people can be pretty weird sometimes. Isaac started asking to spend the night at Sue's and while he did that I saw a calendar pinned to a bulletin board next to the fridge. It had the dates in the month, but underneath each date was a moon. Sometime it was a full circle, sometimes a half, and sometimes a crescent shape like a smile turned sideways.

"Roger, what's this calendar?" I asked.

"Oh, that is what you call a moon calendar, Worm. You can use it to know what phase the moon is going to be in. Take today. It's going to be a three-quarter moon and then tomorrow a full moon. Means the sky will be very bright. Unless we get more of that nasty fog. Sure was something last night wasn't it?"

But I had stopped listening when he said full

moon. Sue and Isaac had come to my side, and now all three of us stared at the calendar. We had two nights before it would be a full moon. Two nights before our new neighbor might try and eat us all in his werewolf form.

CHAPTER 3

Roger had stopped making his fruit fly stuff and walked up to us. "You guys seem to be getting a big kick out of this. Is it the full moon coming up?"

We nodded our heads slowly.

He said, "Did you know that each month there's a full moon, and they all have different names. Take June for instance. You call that moon a honey moon. Or this month's, July's, is called the thunder moon. Kind of spooky, huh?"

He had no idea.

After we left Isaac's grandpa's house we went back to the Secret Hideout. We had secured permission from all the necessary adults. Sue's dad had been cool with us all staying the night, but was a little concerned about us in the Secret Hideout as it had been so foggy the night before. We told him if it got too foggy we would head inside, and we weren't lying, either. No way was I staying outside if it got even a little bit foggy. A werewolf was bad enough; a werewolf that could hide in the fog was extra bad. I remember something Mrs. Henderson used to say when things were going badly. She would say with that big southern accent it was a "hot mess." I couldn't think of anything more of a hot mess than a werewolf on the loose in our neighborhood while a dense fog rolled in. Unless you added a vampire. A vampire, a werewolf, and a dense fog. Hot mess.

Turned out we had nothing to fear regarding the fog. The night was extremely bright because of the three-quarter moon and there was no fog at all. We waited till we saw the light in Sue's dad's room go out, letting us know he had gone to bed, and then we executed Spy Plan Omega Zero. Sue had come up with this name, too, but it was way better than *Spy Book*.

Spy Plan Omega Zero had Sue and me staying in the Secret Hideout with one walkie talkie, while Isaac would sneakily make his way to Mrs. Henderson's old house. Once there he would radio in an all clear to us, and then I would make my way to Isaac's position. Sue would stay at the Secret Hideout prepared to offer backup if anything went wrong. We had two plans in the event the werewolf attacked us. If it attacked us and captured us with the plan of taking us inside the house and conducting experiments on us, Sue would enter in with a baseball bat and save us.

If the werewolf attacked us and started eating us alive, Isaac would radio on the walkie talkie with the code word "desperado." If that happened Sue would instantly call the police and/or her dad from the Secret Hideout and hopefully they would come in time to kill the beast and cut us out from inside his belly. If we did indeed die from being eaten by the werewolf, Isaac and I both agreed there were far worse fates, such as marrying Tiffany Green or having Todd kill us with worm poisoning. Quick aside here. After Roger had told us about the different moon names we looked it up to see if he was messing with us about the thunder moon thing. Turns out he was 100% correct. There's even a worm moon!

The Native Americans named the moons, and they called the full moon in March the worm moon in honor of how many worms would appear as the ground thawed with spring. I thought it was pretty cool that Native Americas thought worms were awesome enough to name an entire moon after them. Please don't ever tell

Todd I said this—or anyone else for that matter—but worms are apparently pretty awesome.

Anyway, the first part of Spy Plan Omega Zero went perfectly. Isaac made his way over to the house and walkie talkied us from the side of Mrs. Henderson's old house. Now it was my turn. I climbed down the rope of the Secret Hideout and waited to hear Sue lock the trap door. We had decided her locking the door was smart on a couple different levels. First, both Isaac and I knew the combination if we needed to get back in. Second, if the werewolf got us it was possible that it might try and get Sue. It only knew my name, but if it had any brains it would figure out quickly about Sue and Isaac.

I was halfway to Mrs. Henderson's when a *huge* thought ran through my head. I ran back to the Secret Hideout and had Sue radio Isaac back. I told them there was a huge error in our thinking. Undoubtedly you already figured this out, and we should have as well. The only excuse I can make is that we weren't sitting safely reading a book like you. We were living in mortal fear of our new neighbor that we were at least 88.5% sure was a werewolf.

"Guys," I said with Sue and Isaac standing around me within the safety of the Secret Hideout. "We don't have anything to fear tonight."

They looked at me like I had just grown two giants zits on my forehead that could talk and play the banjo. "We've been forgetting a super big fact about werewolves!"

I held out my hands, willing Isaac and Sue to come up with the answer on their own. It took a minute and you could see both of them were thinking really hard when suddenly Isaac's eyes lit up. "It's not a full moon!"

He had it right. The full moon was tomorrow.

There would be no werewolf to fear tonight. A person infected with werewolf blood could only turn into a werewolf during a full moon. Otherwise they were normal people just like everyone else. This fact changed everything, and we no longer needed Sue to stay behind for backup. We all climbed down the rope together and made our way to Mrs. Henderson's house.

Now don't get me wrong, we were still plenty nervous and maybe even a little scared. Our neighbor still had werewolf blood running through his veins, and he would want to protect his secret, meaning if he caught us we were probably done for. But for tonight he would be in man shape and we felt pretty confident we could outrun him in case he caught us snooping. After all everyone knows adults are pretty slow runners.

We headed out again, making our way to Mrs. Henderson's old house quietly, still doing our best to stay in spy mode. We would duck behind bushes and hide behind trees whenever possible. When we were about halfway to the house I thought I heard a noise come from some bushes not too far from where we were standing and stopped dead in my tracks to listen. Sue and Isaac had kept walking because they didn't hear anything.

I waited just a few moments and didn't hear anything else so I kept walking and didn't bother telling them about the noise, but I made sure to put all of my senses on red alert status. The last thing we needed was someone or something sneaking up on us. It's possible that even though the neighbor wouldn't be in full werewolf mode until tomorrow that he still was able to utilize some of his werewolf powers, like super stealth or super hearing. As we walked closer to Mrs. Henderson's old house I realized we should have done more research on werewolves. We knew the basic facts, but that was all.

We came upon the house, and the first thing we noticed was that all the lights were off. Not even the porch light was on. Whatever was inside liked darkness and didn't want to provide any light for snooping kids. Sue pulled us aside and was discussing if we should go back and get flashlights when all of a sudden light poured out from a small window that was almost eye level with the ground.

"Basement light just turned on," Isaac whispered and pointed at the window.

"We should check it out," I said.

"Yep. Let's do it." Sue replied. We immediately dropped down onto our bellies and army crawled our way toward the window. If you haven't ever army crawled before what you do is lay down on your belly. You spread out your arms and legs as if you were trying to do a jumping jack and then you use your elbows and arms to pull yourself forward while you kick out with your legs for extra power. It's a great way to move quickly without being seen.

Within mere minutes we had army crawled our way to the window. We put our faces right up to the glass and with the night surrounding us we looked inside the home of the werewolf.

At first it was hard to see anything. It was a basement window that looked down into the room. We had to get just the right angle to be able to see. Once we did that you could see about half of the room, the rest was blocked from view.

In the middle of the room was a long wooden table, like a workmen's bench. On either side of the table stood stuffed animals. Not the kind you would have in your room to hold, like Sue's stuffed octopus Ralph, but the kind that once used to be real animals. One was the big black bear and the other was a lion. The lion had a large mane of hair surrounding its head and teeth even bigger than the bear's.

I hoped that the werewolf wasn't also some type of witch who could make the stuffed animals come alive and do his bidding. Isaac poked me in the ribs with his elbow and said, "I bet those are both animals he hunted when he was in werewolf form and now he keeps them as trophies."

That was much more realistic than the witch idea I had been thinking, and I nodded my head. Sue then shushed us and pointed through the window. We looked back and saw the shadow of a man. The angle of the window blocked us from seeing his face, but we could see from his shoulders down. He was carrying something and he stopped right at the workbench and put it down.

It was something furry all rolled up, like a sleeping

bag made of animal fur. Except it was no sleeping bag, and as he rolled it out we could see that it was the furry skin of a white bear, like a polar bear. The furry skin took up the entire workbench and you could tell that the animal that once wore this fur had been massive. Sue, Isaac, and I all looked at each with our mouths open. We weren't just dealing with a werewolf here. If this thing could kill something as big as that polar bear we were in serious trouble. We looked back at the window and saw that the man now held within his hand what looked like some weird baseball bat, but it was shorter than a bat and thicker around at the end.

"His beating stick," I said. And no sooner had I uttered those words than he took the stick and started striking the fur. When he hit it dust would come floating off the bear fur and fill the air.

It was at that moment as I looked into the

basement room of the werewolf with its dust clouding the air like magic pixie dust let loose from some fairy that the noise I heard earlier sounded again from directly behind us. This time Sue and Isaac heard it as well and we turned around and less than four feet away was a small animal with white circles around its eyes. It hissed at us like a cat, but this was no cat.

It had sharp teeth that you could see when it hissed and its body was all wrong for a cat. Isaac screamed.

"That's nothing to be afraid of," Sue said. "It's just Charlie. He's a raccoon. My dad saw him last year, and we named him. He was just a baby then, and my dad and I left milk for him on the porch. You can see its Charlie by the small scar he has on his right leg."

Isaac and I squinted at his leg and sure enough there was a pen-sized scar there. "Stop hissing, Charlie,"

Sue said and wouldn't you know it, the raccoon listened.

Just then we heard a noise come from the porch and a man's voice shouted out, "Is someone there?"

We took off running toward the back of the house and jumped into some bushes. Now hidden deep in the bushes we turned and looked back and standing there in the darkness with only the little bit of light coming from the basement window to surround him was the man we had seen unrolling the bear skin. It was our new neighbor, the werewolf. It was still too dark to make out his face, but you could tell he was tall. Very tall. He was looking right at us in the bushes and again I wondered if while in man form he could still use his werewolf vision.

Then suddenly we heard Charlie the raccoon hiss again. Charlie hadn't moved at all and was just a few feet from the man. The man looked at Charlie and said, "A raccoon. Huh. Well, we can't have a raccoon running around on the loose." And he made a grab for Charlie, but Charlie saw it coming and skittered away.

Sue whispered, "Good job, Charlie. Run. Run fast."

The man looked at Charlie as he took off and said, "Don't worry, raccoon. I'll catch you tomorrow night." Then he turned around and walked back inside his house.

Sue, Isaac, and I all knew exactly what the man had meant. Tomorrow, during the thunder moon he would turn into a werewolf and hunt Charlie. He would probably kill him and then turn him into a stuffed animal for his collection.

We made our way out of the bushes and ran back to the Secret Hideout. Once back inside we went right to our sleeping bags. The events of the night had left us all feeling pretty tired and the stress of dodging werewolves can really take it out of you. No one said anything, and I was almost asleep when I heard Sue say to herself, "We're going to save Charlie."

That next morning we woke up knowing it might be the last morning of our lives. The werewolf would be coming that night when the thunder moon rose above our neighborhood. It seemed fitting that as we made our way outside the Secret Hideout we saw that storm clouds had filled up the sky. It wasn't raining yet, but it was only a matter of time, and from the looks of the clouds once it started raining it would be one major downpour.

The last time it had rained Sue, Isaac, and I had built boats out of newspapers and sailed them down the gutter. I had named my boat The U.S.S. *Harpoon* and had attached a string with a paperclip that would act as a real life harpoon. How simple and wonderful life had been back then.

As I sat there looking at the cloudy sky and thinking of the werewolf I wished I had taken better advantage of the great moments as they had passed us by. It's easy to look back on one's life when the end is near and think how much more you should have played and laughed.

We decided to have ice cream for breakfast, after all odds were it would be the last breakfast we ever had and why waste it eating something nutritional. Isaac even went and added extra hot fudge. I didn't blame him at all, not one bit.

Sue had found a book of monsters her dad had given her a few years ago. Sue's dad never ever bought Sue a single girly gift, which was fine with Sue because she ended up with some pretty cool things like when she got a pack of bottle rockets for getting all As on her report card or the remote controlled racing car she got when she remembered to do all of her chores one month without being reminded. Sue couldn't remember why she had been given the monster book, but she was glad to have it now.

She thumbed through it, talking as she came across each monster. "Vampire, nope. Zombies, we wish. Everyone knows they are super slow. Frankenstein, *please*. I never understood what's even scary about Frankenstein. Aliens . . ."

We all looked at Isaac. He just shook his head. We have been waiting forever to find out about the aliens from Isaac's grandpa, but so far he had been hush-hush on the subject. Sue continued, "Flesh Eating Jelly Blobs. As if . . . ahh, here we go. Werewolves."

She began reading. Most of it we had already covered, the full moon, the hairy arms, etc. etc. and then it said something Sue, Isaac, and I did not know.

> The werewolf is one of the most
> menacing monsters to walk the earth, and
> taking one down for good is no easy task.
> But if you find yourself facing the
> werewolf all you have to do is arm
> yourself with some silver. Silver burns a
> werewolf and is the only way to kill one.
> Most werewolf hunters arm themselves
> with silver bullets, but this isn't necessary.
> Any silver, even a silver ring or silver
> spoon can be just as effective.

"Yes!" We all yelled, and then I said, "And I know exactly what we can use!" With that we all ran to my house.

I bolted through the front door, past the living room, hurtling over the couch like an Olympian track and field star into the kitchen.

My mom had two silverware sets. There was the fake nice ones we used every day, and there was the one she had been given by my grandma that was made of pure silver! This one was kept high up in the cupboards above the fridge, and we had never eaten with them. Mom said it was too nice and expensive to use, which makes no sense to me. Why have nice stuff if you don't plan on using it? Adults are strange.

I climbed the counter and grabbed the box that safeguarded the silverware. It was super heavy. Way heavier than it looked. I carried it down, and we huffed up to my room with it. Once up there we closed my door and put the box on my bed. It was made of dark red wood, mahogany I think my mom had said, and just looking at the box you could tell that something valuable was inside.

I opened the lid and there lying before us like some ancient pirate treasure were 86 of the highest quality silver spoons, forks, and table knives you have ever seen. Isaac picked up a fork, Sue a knife, and I grabbed the shiniest silver spoon. I held it up to my face; it was so shiny I could see my reflection in it. We held the spoon, knife, and fork above our heads and clinked them together.

I looked in each of their eyes and knew that this would not be our last day on the planet. Armed with our silver eating utensils we were ready to take down the werewolf and save both Charlie and ourselves. The neighborhood might never be allowed to know that we vanquished the terror that lived among us, but we would and that was satisfaction enough.

CHAPTER 4

A minute later, with the silver in our pockets we started making our way downstairs. We were just at my door when a serious of events changed forever how that day should have gone down. Rather than have time to sit in the Secret Hideout and build werewolf traps and practice sword fighting with our silver utensils my mom grabbed me by the shoulder and told me that I would be coming with her and Todd. She didn't say it meanly or anything like that, but she said it that way moms can do that lets you know arguing will be of no use.

She politely asked Sue and Isaac to wait for me and that I would be back shortly. Then with Todd also in tow we walked out of front door. I had no clue what was happening, but I could tell by Todd's expression he wasn't happy, either.

After my mom, Todd, and I had walked to the edge of our house my mom said, "I thought we would bring cookies to our new neighbor and welcome him to the neighborhood."

I stopped dead in my tracks. My mom was about to take Todd and me into the lair of the werewolf and GIVE HIM COOKIES! I couldn't believe it. Adults are so clueless sometimes! I searched for something to say, anything to prevent this from happening. I could just see the werewolf neighbor answer the door and say, "Thank you for the cookies. Why don't you come in, I'd like to have *you* for dinner!"

Todd turned back and said, "Look Mom, Worm is too scared."

"Stop that, Todd," she said to my older brother and then turned to me.

"You too, Hank. Quit playing games. I don't know what gets into you sometimes. Start moving right now, young man."

When my mom says "young man," that's the equivalent to a police officer shouting "Freeze!" You listen or else you're probably going to be shot. I quickly weighed my options and thought that being shot by mom was a worse death than being eaten alive by the werewolf. Besides, maybe he would eat Todd first and there would be some comfort in that.

I continued walking and soon we stood right at Mrs. Henderson's old door. My mom rang the bell and we stood there. Nothing happened. She rang the bell again with no response. I said, "Looks like he's not home, Mom. We better just leave the cookies." And I turned to walk (maybe run) home.

My mom replied, "Nonsense, Hank. I see his red car outside. Maybe the doorbell isn't working." Then she knocked on the door three times. Loudly.

Moments later the door started to open, and I was face to face with our new neighbor the werewolf. Of course he was in normal human form, but I took one look at the hair on his arms and noticed the beard that surrounded his face and all my suspicions were confirmed: Werewolf, all day long.

Other than the hairy arms, which I have to admit weren't that hairy, but hairy enough and the beard he was a pretty average looking adult. He wore a gray shirt and a pair of regular jeans. His face was plain except for the beard. If you met him walking at the hardware store you would think, well this guy seems normal enough. Only the extremely trained eye would know that hidden behind that gray shirt and beard was one of the deadliest monsters that walk earth.

He looked first at me, then at Todd, then to Mom and his eyes settled back on me. "Hank, right?" he asked me. A moment passed, and I made no reply. I stared back at him as he looked at me and fear crept through every bone in my body. Yep, he had heard my mom call out my name that night of the fog when he had first arrived in my neighborhood. As he looked at me I thought I saw his eyes turn red. It might have been some trick of the sun, but I think it was his werewolf vision marking me for his next meal.

Without me ever answering he turned to my mom and said, "Sorry I was so slow getting to the door. I was down in the basement working."

"Oh don't worry about it at all. We just wanted to welcome you to our neighborhood and offer you some homemade cookies." My mom held out the cookies, and the man took them.

"Well, thank you very much. I haven't had homemade cookies in some time." Of course you haven't, I thought to myself. Too busy eating the flesh off of your neighbors.

My mom introduced herself and Todd. Todd shook the neighbor's hand. Todd loves to suck up to adults. It's his biggest trick, getting them to think he is the best kid ever and then he plays them like fools.

My mom asked the man, "What were you working on downstairs?" Not being super nosy, but Mom nosy. Probably wanted some juicy gossip to share at the next Mom's meeting at the local grocery store. Moms love sharing neighborhood information the way kids love finding quarters on the ground.

Todd answered before the man did, "I bet you

were stuffing some new animal."

My mom pinched Todd on the arm. I should probably mention that my mom is a black belt in pinching. There are rumors circulating that she trained under a Tibetan Monk who taught her the long forgotten art of the Dragon Pinch. If Todd or I step out of line she will throw down a pinch on us that will hurt more than being shot by a bazooka. Perhaps even more amazing than the pain of the pinch is that she has long mastered the art of the hidden pinch meaning that her pinches will leave no mark so if Todd or I ever thought about turning her in to child protective services we would never be able to prove anything.

Todd yelped at the pinch, and the man laughed. "Nothing like that I'm afraid, young man. I was just working on building a raccoon trap. Seems we have one on the loose."

"That explains the trash!" my mom said. "Just the other day we had an animal knock down our trash can and chew into a bunch of our garbage."

I couldn't believe my mom was blaming the trash on Charlie the raccoon when it was obviously this man standing right in front of us who was the culprit.

The man nodded as my mom finished talking about how there were claw marks on some of the bags. Then he said, "Yep. They can be a real menace. I found one outside my basement window last night. Seems he had been spying on me." Then the man looked at me. Kids have the ability to read between the lines, a fact most adults don't recognize. It was plain as day that the man was hinting that he thought something other than just Charlie might have been spying.

The minute my mom had knocked on the door of the man's house I had thrust my hand into my pocket and placed my fingers around the silver spoon hidden there. I had wanted to be prepared in the event that he made a move to attack my mom or me. Todd I probably would have let him eat. Now as the man looked at me I felt compelled to action and without any preconceived thought I reached out of my pocket holding the spoon and thrust it onto the man's forearm. I expected to see his skin burn as the spoon made contact and for him to scream in pain, but instead he just stood there looking extremely puzzled. My mom on the other end went ballistic.

"WHAT IN THE WORLD DO YOU THINK YOU ARE DOING HANK?" and she grabbed the spoon from my hand. "IS THIS MY GOOD SILVER? YOU ARE IN SOME SERIOUS TROUBLE!"

Todd was laughing and said, "Oh, my gosh, Worm! You are insane. You thought he was a werewolf, didn't you?" and he fell to his knees laughing.

The man just looked at us all and said, "Don't be too hard on him. I know boys have pretty wild imaginations and with me being a taxidermist . . . well, boys can come up with some pretty crazy ideas. Though I have to admit I have never been called a werewolf before." And he snickered a little.

I looked at him, and I swear those eyes turned red again. Quickly I figured that the silver must not have hurt him since he wasn't in werewolf form. I had blown it big time! Now he knew that I knew he was a werewolf, plus the way my mom was yelling there was no doubt I was going to be grounded, *and* to top it off she had taken my silver from me leaving me weaponless when the werewolf would attack me tonight.

She apologized over and over again to the man who just laughed it off saying it was no big deal, and then she grabbed my arm and half dragged me back to my house. Sue and Isaac greeted me at the front door where she quickly told them that I was grounded and that they would have to leave. I wasn't even allowed to tell them what happened as my mom marched me straight to my room and slammed the door leaving me inside alone.

I hate admitting this, but in full disclosure of the facts I was on the verge of tears, and in hopes of fighting them off I jumped onto my bed, burying my face into my pillow. That's when I felt something hard underneath. I lifted the pillow up and laying there was one of Sue's walkie talkies.

Almost as soon as I made the discovery I heard Sue talking through it, "Secret Hideout to Grounded Boy. Come in, Grounded Boy."

I smiled. Super friends are incredible. They can take away all the tears you are crying, take away all the fears you have of being eaten alive, and make you feel like the world is a perfect place.

"This is Grounded Boy," I said into the walkie, and then I filled them in on all the events that had just happened at Mrs. Henderson's old house. Isaac thought I was super brave to go in alone with the spoon and Sue came to the same conclusion as I had about it not hurting him because he wasn't in werewolf form. We started developing a plan of attack for that night that we could carry out while I was grounded in my room and I have to say it was pretty darn smart:

    A. It was safe to assume that I would be the number one target of the werewolf.

    B. That meant all we had to do was guard my house and the werewolf would come to us.

C. Isaac and Sue, still armed with silver fork and table knife, would hide in the bushes and wait for the werewolf to arrive.

D. I would sit in my room with the light on and window open making myself seem like an easy target. Basically I was the bait.

E. As the werewolf started climbing the wall to my room, Sue and Isaac would jump from the bushes and with silver in hand, ends its reign of terror forever.

I know, pretty sweet plan, right? But one thing you can never plan on when making plans . . . older stinking brothers. Let me tell you what happened.

The rest of the day I was grounded to my room. Which really wasn't that bad. It had started raining like crazy so we would have been stuck inside anyway and with the walkie talkie I was able to chat with Isaac and Sue all day. I just had to be careful to listen for my mom coming up the stairs so I knew to hide the walkie before she opened the door. At times I found myself watching the rain come down, and I thought back to that day we built the paper boats, but daydreaming always turned into nightmares as I knew that it wasn't safe outside while the werewolf lurked.

I heard thunder in the distance and wondered what would happen to our plans if the rain kept coming down, but no sooner did I have that thought the rain stopped. It was as if with the thunder chased the rain away, and I wondered if it did that to make sure we would all see its moon tonight, the thunder moon.

A few hours passed and right as night was settling in on our neighborhood and the thunder moon began its rise my bedroom door opened and there stood Todd. I've known my brother all my life, and in that time I have learned when he is about to mess with me. His eyes squint a little and his cheeks get reddish. The hair on his head sticks out a little taller as if it wants front row seats to what is about to happen to me. This was one of those moments.

I jumped to attention prepared to defend myself from whatever was about to happen. Todd just stood there looking at me and then, while still staring at me with that evil glare of his, he shouted out, "Mom, I want to take Hank down to our new neighbor's house. I think he should apologize, what do you think?"

Almost as soon as the words had left his mouth I heard my mom reply, "I think that sounds like a great idea, Todd. Thank you for being so thoughtful."

Now there's a true suck up.

Todd smiled at me. I thought about putting up a

fight, shouting back at my mom that she had no clue what she was doing. That she was basically sending her youngest son off to his death. I thought about how the plan was ruined now and that I had to warn Isaac and Sue before Todd threw me into the gnashing teeth of the werewolf, but as I turned to grab the walkie talkie from under my pillow, Todd seized my arm and said, "Come on, Worm. Let's go apologize to the werewolf, I mean, new neighbor."

And he dragged me out of the room. It was the second time I was being dragged by someone bigger than me that day, and I was getting a little tired of it, but I knew fighting was useless. Within moments I found myself walking out the front door of the house with Todd telling my mom we would be right back.

The night had already taken hold, and it was dark out, but the light of the thunder moon was very bright, and I could see Mrs. Henderson's old house right down the street waiting for me. I walked next to Todd and thought about begging him to let me go, but I didn't. If tonight was going to be the end of me, I wouldn't let my ugly older brother have the satisfaction of hearing me beg. I walked tall with my back straight and refused to show any fear.

About half way to the house I saw Isaac and Sue bolt from behind a tree to my left. We made quick eye contact, and they went into stealthy spy mode behind us. I looked at Todd to see if he had seen them, but he was just looking ahead with a huge smile across his face. We took about another ten steps and were just passing the big bushes that Sue, Isaac, and I had hid in that night we first saw the new neighbor in his basement, when I heard a great howl.

It came from inside the bushes. It was unlike

anything I had ever heard before, a strange howl that had traces of a deep disturbing, angry growl within it. I leapt about twenty feet in the air and screamed, knowing that my deepest fears were coming true. I was about to be eaten for sure.

Isaac and Sue disengaged from stealthy spy mode and ran up to me grabbing me by the arms. They were risking their lives in an attempt to pull me away from Todd and whatever was making the howling noise inside the bushes, but we never made it further than that because just as they grabbed me the leaves of the bushes spread apart and out stepped the werewolf.

He had fangs coming out of his mouth and hair all over his arms and legs. He stood tall and looked hungry. He stopped just mere feet away from us and raised his head and howled at the thunder moon. Sue, Isaac, and I screamed louder than I thought was humanly possible, and I'm beyond thankful that I didn't pee my pants, but I was close.

The werewolf took another step toward us and raised his hands above his head as if he was about to pounce on us. We fell to the ground screaming for help when behind the werewolf came a loud hiss. The werewolf turned around from us and there standing on his hind legs was Charlie the raccoon.

Charlie looked ready to pounce and his teeth looked sharp as razor blades with the light of the full moon shining down on them. Even Todd was scared and took a step back and tripped over himself landing hard on his butt. I would have laughed if it hadn't been for the fact that a killer werewolf was just moments away from eating me.

"No Charlie! Don't be a hero! Run, boy!" Sue yelled, but Charlie just stood there hissing at the werewolf. Fearless.

The werewolf made a shooing movement with his arms, the way you will do when you want something to back away, but Charlie didn't budge an inch.

The werewolf turned to Todd and shrugged his shoulders. Todd said, "Just kick the thing, man." Which I thought was a very weird thing for Todd to say, and I found it even weirder that the werewolf was looking to Todd for advice on how to handle a raccoon.

The werewolf turned back to Charlie and raised his leg to strike, but before he could make contact Charlie jumped like a delta force warrior and bit him right in the leg, sinking his teeth deep into the hair covered flesh.

The werewolf cried out. "He bit me, man! Todd, he bit me!" and grabbed down at his leg. Charlie ran off back into the bushes, and now the werewolf was sitting down on the ground grabbing his leg, and I swear I could hear it sobbing. "Oh, man. I bet I got rabies. This was stupid, Todd!" and with that the werewolf reached up and pulled off its face.

It wasn't a werewolf at all! It was Todd's red headed friend Gus Henry.

The night ended right there with Todd rushing back home to get my mom and then all of us driving to the emergency room to make sure that Gus Henry didn't have rabies. The entire drive Sue told Gus to stop being a baby and that he was fine and no way would Charlie have any disease especially rabies. It turned out Sue was right, and Gus was fine.

Todd came clean with my mom and told her that he had Gus dress up in a werewolf costume in an attempt to scare me. Apparently Gus had been a werewolf just last Halloween, so he had the costume on hand. Mom quickly grounded him for an entire week. Ha! The sweet taste of justice.

We came back from the emergency room and the night ended with us all safe in our beds. No one ever saw a real werewolf that thunder moon, but I promise you that as I put my head down on my pillow that night I heard a howl in the distance. From that day forward whenever we walked, ran, or biked across Mrs. Henderson's old house we did it from the other side of the street. We never fully proved that our new neighbor was a werewolf, but it's always better to be safe than sorry when dealing with monsters.

THE BURPDAY PARTY

Throughout the known history of mankind eight people have been born with what is known in certain circles as The Gift of the Cone. I am one of the chosen. I was 184 days old when this gift manifested itself. It was at my horrible older brother Todd's birthday party and the flavor being served was vanilla. My mom says it is impossible for me to remember the flavor ice cream that was served at his party on the account that I wasn't even a year old, but she doesn't understand the gift that I have.

I can recall every single time I have been served the soft deliciousness that is ice cream as well as every flavor I've ever had. It's a gift. Even blindfolded I can tell you the exact flavor of ice cream just by smelling it in the cone. Easy, you say? ha! Try it yourself and see how difficult it really is. Oh sure, any cheeseball can guess vanilla, but can you guess vanilla swirl? Or Strawberry peach? With a single whiff and one whiff alone can you guess butter pecan? Or if you really want to see if you may be one of the chosen you should go to Mr. Jeffries's Ice Cream Parlor.

It is right next to the Science and History Museum downtown and it is *by far* the best ice cream in the entire universe. Mr. Jeffries has been making his own ice cream since the Stone Age. In fact he's been making it for so long my mom used to go there when she was a kid and her mom's mom used to go there and her mom's mom's mom used to go there. I don't know how old Mr. Jeffries is, but he must be at least 250 years old, and normally I wouldn't want a guy that old making me ice cream cones, but Mr. Jeffries is an ice cream artist, and what he can do with ice cream is crazy. He is always inventing new flavors of ice cream, and each new flavor is far better than the last.

For instance last time I went he had taken fudge swirl, added half a scoop of mint chocolate chip, thrown in a partial scoop of bubble gum flavor, added three huge squirts of hot fudge, then mixed in gummy bears. He called it BubbleBEARydelicious and it was like the best thing I had ever tasted.

I once asked him why he keeps making new flavors, and he said, "Worm, I've been searching for the perfect scoop of ice cream my whole life. At times I think I have come close, but the perfect scoop still evades me. It's my white whale."

Two things.

1. Yes – Mr. Jeffries calls me Worm. You can

thank Todd for that. Whenever he gets the chance he convinces every adult that I like the nickname Worm, so more than half of the adults in our town now call me Worm. I tried correcting people, but it takes way more effort than it's worth.

2. I have no clue what the whole "white whale" thing is about. I guess that's what he wants to call the perfect flavor when he finally discovers it, which I think sounds like one of the worst names ever, but people love vanilla ice cream and that's a pretty bad name as well.

Isaac, Sue, and I make it to Mr. Jeffries's Ice Cream Parlor at least twice a month, but there is never a time more cherished than during the Summer Extravaganza.

Each year the Science and History Museum ends the summer with a big bang by bringing in a special exhibit. They call it the Summer Extravaganza.

Now the Summer Extravaganza would be cool enough, but for us it's even more cool because the exact day that it opens, the last Saturday of summer, is also . . . drumroll please . . . Isaac's birthday! It couldn't be more perfect! So each year we get to say goodbye to summer by having the best birthday party ever at the Science and History Museum and see the coolest exhibits ever. Some of the past exhibits at the Summer Extravaganza were:

- Bugs From the Four Corners of the Globe. They brought in humongous giant roaches from Africa and other exotic bugs from all over. The roaches were so big and nasty. Isaac said they reminded him of Todd. I told him that was rude and made him apologize to the roaches. My favorite part was that they had a cricket spitting contest in which you got to take a real cricket and see how far you could spit it. The kid who won it all was named Henry Jacobs. He went to our school and to this very day he keeps the blue ribbon they gave him for coming in first tied to his backpack. I don't blame him at all for showing it off because if I had won I would have had the ribbon framed and probably made my mom put a spotlight on it so that everyone could see it for miles around. Look, for a kid in today's world you get medals and awards for almost everything, you don't even have to win. I have a medal for when I played soccer in kindergarten and our team didn't even win a single game, in fact the only goal we scored all year wasn't in our own net. We

were horrible! But I still have a medal.
They just give these things away, but
Henry Jacobs, man he earned that ribbon.
He spit that cricket over 23 feet!

- Mummies and Tombs. This one was so
  cool! They had mummies, I mean like real
  mummies brought in. These were actual
  dead people from ancient Egypt that had
  been wrapped in Egyptian toilet paper so
  that they wouldn't decompose. When we
  got back from Isaac's birthday party that
  year we wrapped each other in toilet paper
  and pretended we were mummies. It was a
  lot of fun until Todd caught us and
  grabbed the rolls of toilet paper and spun
  them around us over and over again until
  we couldn't move. Then he pushed us

down and laughed while we tried to get out. Sue started crying and her toilet paper started getting all wet and then it stuck to her hair and it took her forever to get it out. To this day if you look closely at her hair, deep in the roots, hiding behind her bangs are traces of white toilet paper.

This year Roger told us that the Summer Extravaganza exhibit was going to be Underwater Adventures. The museum was going to have a complete collection of artifacts from Wild Bill Kelper who had been the world's premier deep diver before he had a tragic scuba diving accident off the coast of Australia.

Roger had bought Isaac a book all about Wild Bill as an early birthday present, and we had all been reading through it the past week as we prepared to see the Summer Extravaganza exhibit. It was so cool learning about Wild Bill and how he got his start as a diver in the Navy. It was his job to dive down to these big underwater bombs called mines and disable the mine so that it couldn't hurt anyone anymore.

Apparently all over the ocean there are mines chained to the sea floor. The book had a picture of one, and it looked like a giant steel ball with big medal spikes pointing out all around it, and there was a huge chain secured to the bottom of the ball to keep it from floating away. These mines had originally been placed by enemy soldiers during a war, and they were designed so that if a submarine or a battleship touched the mine it would explode and take down the ship. The book said hundreds of ships had fallen victim to these mines and that there were still thousands of them hidden all over the ocean floor.

According to Roger there was going to be an

actual mine at the exhibit that we would get to touch!
And if that wasn't enough there was going to be a gigantic
water pool right in the middle of the exhibit where kids
could get into an actual diving suit and go underwater!

The pool was going to be filled with coral and fish
and even a shark, a juvenile nurse shark, which is like a
little shark that won't attack people, but still . . . After
Isaac's birthday I was going to be able to say I had swum
in shark infested waters. Now that is a Summer
Extravaganza!

The night before Isaac's birthday we all stayed the
night at the Secret Hideout. Spending birthday eve at the
Secret Hideout was a time honored tradition that all of
our parents and grandparents respected. Sue's birthday
was in April and often it would fall on a school night—no
biggie. We still spent the night at the Secret Hideout. Two
years ago I had been grounded on my birthday eve for

tracking mud throughout the house—no biggie. We still spent the night at the Secret Hideout.

In fact we figured if there was anything we could do wrong that could possibly prevent our adults from allowing us to spend our birthday eves together and regardless of what idea we came up—the best coming from Sue who threw out the horrible crime of playing water guns in the house while we put a metal spoon in the microwave all the while leaving the fridge door open—we decided that there was indeed no crime that the punishment of separating us during birthday eve would be acceptable.

Isaac's birthday eve was always the hardest to get into the party spirit. You see, even though Isaac has the coolest birthday ever with the opening of the Summer Extravaganza, his birthday still falls near the last day of summer and there are few things in this world more dreadful than the last day of summer. I once wrote a petition to our state senator that the last day of summer should be celebrated as a national holiday and that we should get the first week of school off in observance of it. I'm still waiting for a reply.

As we sat around the table in the Secret Hideout, a half-played game of Monopoly in front of us, I looked around and saw that Sue and Isaac were looking gloomy. Thoughts of schoolwork danced in their heads and no doubt they were lost in the forever gloom of homework assignments and pop quizzes. I felt so bad for Isaac having this cloud of school over his head and decided enough was enough. I slammed my fist down on the table, scattering the monopoly money and even causing the dog piece (Sue is always the dog) to go flying off the table.

"Super Friends! I implore you to take no heed of

the dreaded schooldays that lay before us."

Sue shifted her face down to the table and softly whispered, "It's hard, Hank. Tomorrow is going to be so fun at the Summer Extravaganza, but we'll also get our teacher assignments in the mail. I'm sorry, Isaac. I want to just focus on the fun we are going to have, but it's hard."

Isaac patted Sue on the back. "Don't worry. I feel the same way. We'll be eating ice cream tomorrow at Mr. Jeffries's, but the whole time in the back of my head is going to be school."

School. Oh that terrible word. It enters our life like a plague slowly engulfing everything in its path. Not even a birthday can override the horribleness that comes with the word *school*.

Suddenly I had a thought and that thought grew into a concept and that concept grew into an IDEA. Yes, I had an IDEA. All capitals. Most ideas are lower capital ideas like when we have the idea to play tag or the idea to go for a bike ride, but every now there is an all caps kind of IDEA. Now these IDEAS are the kind that cannot be ignored. George Washington had an IDEA when he fought the red coats for America. Benjamin Franklin had an IDEA when he flew that kite in the lightning storm. Mr. Jeffries had an IDEA when he made BubbleBEARydelicious. And now within my mind was an IDEA that could forever change how we looked at school!

I stood from my chair and began to pace. If you haven't ever paced you haven't ever lived. Pacing is the art form of walking back and forth over and over again. Through the art of pacing all the great speeches are given. If you don't believe me watch some of those old war movies, and you will see that the general always paces as he gives the speech that will motivate his troops to battle.

And I wasn't just pacing. I was speed pacing. I looked like a small tornado flying left, right, left, right, left, right, left right, faster and faster. Sue and Isaac watched me their heads swiveling with me as I moved as if they were watching a tennis match and following the ball as it was hit across the net. Back and forth. Back and Forth. Then I stopped dead in my tracks. Oh my, I had their attention. Their eyes almost bulged right out of their heads. They could feel that the world was about to change.

"Isaac," I said.

"Yeah?" He almost looked scared. He knew something big was about to happen, but that fear that comes when you aren't really sure what is about to happen was all over his face.

"Tell us what your grandpa says about words," I said, my words coming out fast like a train through a dark mountain pass.

"Worms?" he looked dumbfounded.

"No! WORDS?" I said a little slower. I was talking fast like a crazy person. I needed to slow it down.

"Ummm . . . I don't know what he says about words."

Looks like he was going to need some coaxing. "You know what I'm talking about. What does Roger say about words and power?"

His eyes lit up. "Ohhh, I know what you're talking about now. Grandpa says, 'Words have power'."

"Yes, he does! Yes, he does!" I lifted up my pointer finger to the sky as I said it. I was going for a Sherlock Holmes type moment like we had just discovered a major clue. Both Sue and Isaac had seen me make this motion at least a thousand times over the past years, and they responded by nodding their heads up and down. They were with me!

"And he's right, team. Words have power. Big power. Take the words *ice cream*, for instance. What happens when you say them?"

Sue licked her lip., "You get hungry and want some!" And we all laughed as her stomach growled.

"You get what I'm talking about. What about you, Isaac? When I say the word *ninja* what happens?" Isaac immediately made a karate chop motion. "That's right! Just thinking the word *ninja* makes you want to karate chop and do back flips while throwing ninja stars."

Sue looked from Isaac to me. "What does that have to do with going back to school?"

"Don't you see? We've been allowing the word *school* to have power over us."

Isaac jumped up from his chair. "You're right! We've been acting like a bunch of worms every time we hear or think the word *school*."

"Yea. You're right," said Sue. "But what are we going to do about it? I mean I can't help thinking how bad life is going to be when school starts again."

"AGH!" I shouted out and put my hands over my ears. "No more saying that word. For the rest of summer that word is now banned from our lips."

"What word? School?" Isaac said.

"AGH!" I screamed at the top of my lungs. "Yes, THAT word."

Sue smiled as she said, "You mean we shouldn't say *school*?"

"AHHHHH!" I screamed and started laughing. Sue and Isaac laughed as well. After we calmed down and all agreed that we wouldn't say the word *scho*-I mean say *that* word ever again. Isaac asked what we should say when we were wanting to talk about . . . that place. This is the exact question I had been waiting for.

"From now on, when we think or want to talk about the place our teachers work, we'll substitute the word we normally would have said with a word we like. A word that has good power. But what word?"

Isaac brought his fingers to his chin, his thinking pose.

We sat around for a while, and then Sue shouted out, "I got it! From now on instead of saying school—"

"AHHHH!" Isaac and I shouted.

"Sorry," said Sue. "From now on instead of saying *that word*, we'll say pizza."

It was perfect. We spend the rest of the night having the best birthday eve ever and even though every now and then we thought about that pizza we found it didn't bother us and it actually made us smile. Yes pizza was less than three days away and tomorrow we would find out who are teachers were, but no longer did it stop us from having fun. After all who doesn't like pizza?

We woke up early, the sun not even visible yet although you could see the first rays of its light as it stretched out across the sky, and we biked over to Isaac's house thinking we had a chance to actually be up earlier than Roger, something we had tried to do a few times and always fallen short. Old people wake up earlier than the sun rises and Roger was no exception. His space training had taught him to be a light sleeper, meaning that the smallest noise will wake him up, and Roger says that every morning he wakes up to the noise of the moon setting. He smiles when he says this and has this wistful look in his eyes.

I have seen the moon through a telescope, and if you haven't yet you should. It's mesmerizing, and you can go into a moon trance in which you can spend hours looking at the individual craters on the surface of the moon. I can't imagine what the moon trance can do to a man like Roger who has actually set foot on it.

Once over space spaghetti Roger told us about the time he landed on the moon and what it was like to take his first step out of the space ship and look down to see his footprint on the surface of the moon. If you don't have a neighbor who was once an astronaut you should get one. The way you look up at space will change forever.

We sneaked into the house, barely making any noise ever and we crossed our fingers. No doubt this would be the day we finally woke up before him, but as we turned around the kitchen wall we found him there wide awake and making coffee.

"Well, good morning, you late sleepers," he said, smiling at us. "Isaac, Worm, Sue, anyone want any coffee?"

Heads up. If an adult ever asks you if you want to try coffee run away screaming. The only thing nastier than the taste of coffee is kissing Tiffany Green.

"Happy Birthday, Isaac," Roger said and went and gave Isaac a hug. It can be a little embarrassing when an adult gives you a hug in front of your friends so Sue and I, being Super Friends and knowing this, quickly turned away so Isaac wouldn't see us watching.

"Who is ready for some Summer Extravaganza?"

"We are!" the three of us yelled in unison. It was going to be the best day ever—at least that is what we thought.

The official birthday celebration started with a stop to Mr. Jeffries's Ice Cream Parlor. Mr. Jeffries was standing behind the counter as he has been for well over 200 years, by my earlier calculations. When we entered

Isaac whispered that he bet Mr. Jeffries was a vampire, but Sue hissed back that it was impossible because the sun was shining in the shop and everyone knows that sunlight will kill a vampire.

"Well fine," said Isaac. "I'll admit he's not a vampire, but something has to be up. Grandpa says that Mr. Jeffries used to serve him ice cream when he was a kid and that was like 400 years ago."

We all nodded, and I was about to say that maybe he was an immortal sent from a distant planet to watch earth and keep it safe from evil aliens, but before I got this out Mr. Jeffries called out to us. "Hey Worm, hi Sue, and HAPPY BIRTHDAY, ISAAC!"

"Hi, Mr. Jeffries," we called back to him. We ran to the counter and looked at all the flavors, the only thing separating the delicious taste of ice cream from our hungry faces was the two inch thick sheet of glass. We were so close that our mouths left a vapor fog. I wiped away the fog with the sleeve of my shirt and stared at the cold goodness that lay before me like an ice cream buffet. There were sherbets of every color, strawberry chunk, vanilla (boring, yet still yummy), bubble gum, red apple, double Dutch chocolate chip, mint chocolate chip, raspberry, rocky road, birthday cake with real bits of cake hidden inside, peanut butter swirl, cookies and cream, and so much more. Mr. Jeffries's Ice Cream Parlor has every single flavor under the sun.

I was in ecstasy, and life had culminated into perfection, when behind me the bell that hangs above the door and rings when someone walked in chimed. I didn't really register the noise as I was lost in ice cream land, but the voice that followed it violently ripped me away from my joy.

"Oh Mom, look! It's Hank!" And I turned around

I saw her. Tiffany Green. Her eyes met mine, and I could tell she was trying to put a love spell on me. I looked away fast. She walked up to me. "Hi Sue, hi Isaac." But even as she said it I would bet she never took her eyes off me.

She turned toward the ice cream and saw the vapor fog that Isaac had made. He hadn't yet wiped his away as I had. She took her finger and traced out a heart and then inside it she wrote the letters HAT. Hank and Tiffany. Ugh. I took my sleeve and erased the letters as fast as I could, but no matter how much I rubbed you could still see the trace of them. Tiffany smiled and walked to Mr. Jeffries.

"Hello, Tiffany," he said.

"Hello, Mr. Jeffries. May I have two scoops of Love Berry?" And she turned to me smiling. Double ugh.

"Coming right up, Miss Green."

"I just love Love Berry, don't you, Hank? It's got strawberry flavored ice cream with little heart candies. If you want I'll share it with you?" Triple disgustoid ugh.

"Hurry up, Tiffany, we need to get to the spa for our appointment," Tiffany's mom said from the door, looking at her watch.

Tiffany took her cone from Mr. Jeffries and said to me, "Maybe next time, Hanky Panky." And she turned and left.

Sue, Isaac, and I immediately began acting like we were throwing up.

Roger laughed and said, "Well, Worm, at least you know there's one out there for you if you ever change your mind." And Mr. Jeffries and he laughed some more.

"No, thank you," I said. Knowing I needed to change the subject before they made any more dumb adult jokes I turned toward Mr. Jeffries and brought up the perfect flavor. "Any luck on the perfect flavor?"

He looked down at all the flavors before him and shook his head no. Then he looked up at me almost with a tear in his eye and said, "Not yet, Worm. I thought I was onto something the other day with a mix of Neapolitan, peach cobbler, and chocolate swirl, but alas the perfect flavor still eludes me."

Then he looked at Isaac and brightened up. "But Isaac, I was thinking of your birthday and knew you and the gang would all be coming by. I called up Roger on the phone, and together we came up with something special just for you guys. We call it Outer Space Moon Madness. Would you guys like to try it?"

We moved our heads up and down so fast that the world around us became a blur.

"I thought so," said Mr. Jeffries, and with that we watched as he started scooping.

Moments later all of us had in our hands the splendor of Outer Space Moon Madness. I would tell you the ingredients, but Mr. Jeffries swore us to secrecy. All I can say is that it's so good that I completely forgot all about Tiffany Green and found perfect balance with the world again.

We left the ice cream parlor with our bellies full of delicious goodness and walked toward the Museum of Science and History where the artifacts of Wild Bill Kelper and the water pool awaited us. If only we had known what was going to happen in the next few hours we might have walked a little slower, but we didn't, and instead we skipped and ran as fast as we could to the museum.

As we entered the doors we were immediately surrounded by the Wild Bill exhibit. Standing right before us was the actual dive suit he had worn on his Navy dives.

It was a ghostly white suit with large orange gloves. The helmet was made of copper metal with glass on all four sides. There was a giant hose coming from the top of the helmet, and it was this hose that provided him air from above as he made his dives. The boots on the suit were made of the same copper metal and must have weighed a hundred pounds.

All three of us stared at the suit and imagined what it must have been like to be Wild Bill Kelper diving into the middle of the ocean. Sharks coming from every side. A harpoon in hand to knock them away as you slowly fell further and further down into the depths of the sea. It would become darker as the sun stopped penetrating the water, and you would have to turn on your helmet light to see even a few feet in front of you.

We looked back up at the suit and right there attached to the side of the helmet was the light we were just imagining. He really did it! And oh, I knew I could, too. I could see the cold water surrounding me with just my helmet light on, giant fish with sharp teeth swimming by. Then out of nowhere a giant squid as big as a bus would wrap its tentacles around my leg trying to pull me down to my doom. I would use the harpoon and stab at the beast and just as I thought I couldn't win it would let go. I would wonder why and turn around and there inches away would be a giant mine left by the enemy years ago.

We walked further into the museum and there on the floor was one of the actual mines Wild Bill had disarmed. Sue was the first to walk up and touch one of the spikes that poked out of the metal ball. We had been told it was disarmed and all the explosive bomb parts had been removed, but as she touched it we all tensed up in case they were wrong and we were all about to be blown to pieces. Nothing happened though, and Isaac and I walked up next to touch it ourselves. I could just see Wild Bill reaching out and touching it years ago when it was still armed and dangerous.

We read the plaque next to the mine and it told us that what Wild Bill had to do was go underneath the mine and unscrew a large plate that was on the bottom. From there the piece that triggered the bomb would slide out, and Wild Bill would have to cut the exact right wires to disarm the mine.

Roger let us roam free the rest of the way and down a couple corridors we found the middle of the mine that Wild Bill would've had to unscrew out. It was a large cylinder of metal full of rust, and there were wires coming out from all over. Some were green, others red or yellow. Next to this artifact there was a sign that said each mine was armed a little differently so that Wild Bill would have to work through each wire to determine the exact right one to cut. Incredible.

I turned to Isaac and Sue to say how awesome Wild Bill was when out of the corner of my eye I caught sight of my horrible older brother Todd. I elbowed Sue and pointed. She gasped and in term elbowed Isaac and pointed. He gasped and elbowed me and pointed. I then elbowed Sue again, she elbowed Isaac again, and we started laughing. Then we remembered why we had been elbowing in the first place and quickly stopped laughing.

Todd is the worst enemy, and if he noticed us who knew what would happen, but our luck was holding up, and Todd didn't see us. He was standing next to a big door a ways down the hall. Gus was right next to him, and they were kind of hunched over talking in secret. Then Todd reached up turned the knob to the door, and Gus and he slipped behind it. It closed loudly, and I saw a security guard of the museum go toward it. He opened the door and looked inside. I guess Todd and Gus had a good hiding spot because after looking in for a few seconds the guard stopped and let the door close. Then he just stood by the door and started whistling.

Sue said, "What was that about?"

"I don't know," I replied. "Let's go check it out." With that we started down hall, and as we got closer we saw a big sign on the door that read OFF LIMITS. AUTHORIZED PERSONNEL ONLY. When we got close to the door the guard said, "Sorry kids. This part of the exhibit is off limits. You guys aren't allowed back here."

We said no problem and turned around and walked back to where we were.

"Well, looks like Todd is breaking the rules again," Isaac said.

"Yep. I wonder what he's up to," I said.

"I don't know, and it's totally chapping my hide." Every now and then when Sue gets upset she drops into all out cowboy mode.

Her grandpa was originally from Texas and was a famous rodeo champion. He had won 17 different rodeos before he hurt his knee one day riding a bull named Monster Jack Flash and had to turn in his cowboy chaps and settle down.

He would come visit Sue sometimes, and he said the coolest cowboy stuff. Isaac, Sue, and I kept a journal where we would write down some of the things he said so we wouldn't forget it. Here are just a few of them:

A. Don't squat with your spurs on.

B. Always take a good look at what you're about to eat. It's not so important to know what it is, but it's critical to know what it was.

C. Just 'cause trouble comes visiting doesn't
    mean you have to offer it a place to sit down.

D. If you get thrown from a horse, you have to
    get up and get back on, unless you landed on
    a cactus, in which case you have to roll
    around and scream in pain.

Isaac spoke next saying, "The only thing worse than when Todd captures us is when we knew he is doing something sneaky, but we don't know what it is."

"I know. I know. But what can we do? We can't go in that room with that security guard standing watch," I said.

Sue snapped her fingers. "Time for a plan."

We talked through a couple of different strategies, each one more dangerous than the one before when suddenly Sue snapped her fingers again. She told us her plan, and it was great! We huddled around each other and placed our hands in the middle.

"Super Friends on three," I said and then counted. "1, 2, 3 . . . Super Friends!"

"Time to execute plan Lost Child." Then Sue walked toward the security guard while Isaac and I hid behind an exhibit of Wild Bill's personal letters. We could hear Sue start crying from our hiding spot.

We leaned out from behind the exhibit and saw the security guard put his hand on Sue's shoulder and ask her what was wrong.

In between sobs Sue said, "I lost my brother." Sob. Sob. "He was right behind me and then all of the sudden he was gone." More sobbing. "He said he wanted to go to the diving pool, but I don't know where that is. I'm scared for him." Big sob.

The guard took her by the hand and said, "No problem. I'll take you there right now." And with that Sue and the security guard left.

With Sue in full sob diversion mode Isaac and I ran to the door for stage two of the plan. I was a little nervous about opening the door. I saw that big sign with the red letters OFF LIMITS, but before I could think too much about it, Isaac opened the door. He looked back at me. "We have no choice. For all we know Todd is about to do something terrible. I mean he might be planning some kind of global domination scheme. We have to stop him."

Obviously he was right. If there was anyone capable of global domination it is Todd. Without further thought, I walked with Isaac into the room, letting the door close behind me.

The first thing I noticed was that it was pretty dark. There was one big box to the left and no doubt Gus and Todd had hidden behind it waiting for the guard to leave. Isaac and I walked toward the back of the room, careful in case Todd was hiding somewhere waiting for us. There really wasn't much to see: a couple of small boxes, some things with dusty sheets covering them up, and a big pole with a hook on the end on the ground. We weren't really sure what Todd was after or where he could have gone. There were no other doors.

I told Isaac we needed to secure the perimeter and do a thorough search. We each took a different side of the room and walked along the wall. We looked for trap doors or secret passages, but found nothing.

"Man, Hank. Where did they go?"

"I have no clue." And with a large exhale I sat down on the floor. He sat next to me and laid down exhausted from the search. Immediately after he laid down he shouted out, "Look there!" I looked up and way above us was a hole in the ceiling. We never would have found it if we hadn't laid down first. Coming out of the hole were a couple rungs of a ladder, but it was way too high for anyone to reach up and grab.

"Great work!" I said. "But how did they get up there?"

"See, flying is the best super power." And so it began once again. For over five years Isaac, Sue, and I have had an ongoing debate about which is the best super power. All this time Isaac has held onto flying as the supreme power. I personally am an invisibility man. I mean come on, what possible power could come in handier than invisibility? A teacher about to pass out a pop quiz? Boom! Invisibility. Tiffany Green has you cornered on the playground? Boom! Invisibility. Todd is about to grab you and throw you into a vat of worms. You got it, invisibility. Sue is a super strength person. She believes that super strength is by far the best super power.

Imagine being able to lift a car or train or even an entire house. I admit it's a cool power, but it's not invisibility. I mean heck, having money troubles? Become the world's best bank robber with the power of invisibility, but I did have to admit that at the moment with that ladder way out of reach that Isaac's flying would have been a sweet super power.

I was just about to say this to him when I once again noticed the pole on the ground and realized exactly what it was there for.

"Check this out," I said and lifted the pole so that the hook on the end reached up and grabbed the last rung of the ladder.

I tried to pull it down with the hook, but it wouldn't move. Isaac came over and together we tugged as hard as we could, and just when we thought it wouldn't budge, the ladder gave way and slid all the way down to the floor. Now we could easily climb up and see what Todd was up to.

"Isaac, before we go up there I want to say something."

"What?"

"Happy Birthday. I just wanted to make sure to tell you that in case the worst happens to us up there."

Isaac grabbed my hand and shook it. We looked up one last time and then taking hold of all the bravery a kid can have we started climbing up.

Soon we were at the top of the ladder, and the hole opened up to reveal a walking platform suspended from the roof. I knew immediately what it was.

"Look! It's a catwalk."

"What's that?"

"I saw one of these during a tour of the Chesterfield Playhouse. See a lot of times during plays they have guys who walk up on these so they can see the play happening below. They can pull levers up here and move the sets below or have a bucket of water that they can turn over and spill on the actors to make it look like its raining."

"That's cool." We started walking down the platform. "But why would they have a catwalk here at the museum?"

"I don't know, but look down. It's the diving pool!" And with that we both looked down and could see about 30 feet below us was the diving pool.

We could see the fish swimming around and then all of a sudden we saw the shark swim by. It was awesome! We could also look out at the crowd below and see a long line of kids waiting for their turn to get into the diving suit and go into the water.

"Hey, look," Isaac said, pointing down to the

crowd. "There's Sue." And sure enough there was Sue. She was standing next to the pool looking around. When she was making the plan she had said we would use the diving pool as our meeting point, and it was obvious watching her that she was waiting for us. We were just about to shout down to her when we felt the catwalk move beneath our feet. We looked up and there standing just a few feet away were Todd and Gus.

"Looky here, Gus. Looks like Worm and his pal have found our secret spot." I won't lie to you. I was scared. Todd had that look on his face when the worst of the worst was about to happen.

The last time he had that look on his face was three years, five months, and ten hours before when he had gotten the hair clippers from my mom's room and he shaved my head saying that worms don't have hair. Which is actually wrong. Some worms do have hair on their bodies called setae. You can't really see it, but if you ever stroke a worm from tail to front you can easily feel the hair. Like I have said before, I have learned an awful lot about worms over the years.

As Isaac and I stood frozen in place the exact same look as that fateful day of hair loss was all over Todd's face, and it must have been contagious because soon Gus had the same look.

"Hey, Gus, do you think worms can fly?" And even as the words left his mouth Todd started running toward us.

This is the part of the story where I would love to tell you that we turned and ran escaping the clutches of my evil brother or that we raised our fists and scared him and Gus away with our intense faces and muscular strength, but instead we just stood there frozen in fear.

CHAPTER 2

Seconds later Todd had me by the ankles and was

hanging me over the rail of the catwalk, dangling me like

some flag in the wind. I was freaking out as I stared at the

water below me with the shark swimming around.

Somewhere in the back of my mind I knew that it was

just a harmless juvenile nurse shark, but at that exact

moment in time it became a great white to me. I thought

if Todd dropped me I would be eaten alive by this

underwater monster, my blood and guts floating in the

pool as kids and parents screamed in horror.

I looked up and saw that Gus had grabbed hold

of Isaac and he was powerless to help me in my plight.

This would be the end of my adventures. Todd the Barbarian had won and with one swallow of the mighty shark all traces of my existence would be forever gone, wiped from the earth like a footprint on the beach as the tide rolls in. I started to scream and wail. I won't pretend here, my friends, I sounded like the death screams of a drowning giraffe.

"I'm just messing with you, Worm. I wouldn't drop yo—" And then Todd lost his grip of my right leg.

I believe him. I don't think he intended to actually drop me, but as my right leg became free I slipped out of his grip entirely and began my descent into the pool.

If you haven't ever been dropped by your older brother from a catwalk 30 feet above a diving pool infested with marine wildlife and complete with a shark here is what goes through your mind:

1. This can't be happening. I have done some research and this is a pretty common thought that goes through the mind of someone falling into a shark pool. Apparently your mind is trying to convince itself that there is no way in the universe that this could *really* be happening to you, and it's trying to wake you up from your apparent nightmare.

2. Oh no, this is really happening. This is the second thought, and research again points this is an expected thought response to the situation. All in all thoughts 1 and 2 happen in less than a second and then thoughts really get interesting as your mind and body come together to prepare for your inevitable doom.

3. Look, there's Sue. My mind was able to register during my flight down all of the

surroundings below. It is incredible the clarity at which I was able to see into the shark pool: the beautiful coral, the salt water fish full of stripes and bright colors, but also I could see the people outside the pool that were standing around doing normal museum things and not falling into a death pool. It was as if time slowed down during my descent and my eyes became extra observant. I could see a tall mom in a yellow shirt holding the hand of a toddler who was bending over to pick up a stuffed elephant. Behind the mom in yellow were two teenage girls texting away on their phones. No doubt OMGs and IDKs were being typed in rapid fire succession. And then to the left of them was Sue.

4. Super Friend look up. I did not say this out loud only thought it, but the link that bonds Super Friends exists on both a physical level and telepathic level, and no sooner had I thought this then Sue looked up. I could see her eyes bulge out, and I thought it was possible they were going to jump right off her face like a cartoon's. To have one of her Super Friends become shark meat *and* go blind all at the same time is more than anyone should have to face. Luckily Sue's eyes decided to stay attached to her face, and I could see them move from me to the crowd surrounding the pool.

5. What is she thinking? It's an odd thought to think about what others are thinking while you are thinking as you fall to your certain

death. Yet, that's what I thought, and Sue answered the question at about 18 feet 3 inches from the pools surface. She yelled loudly and started running in circles. All of the attention moved from the diving pool and was directed toward her. The only people who didn't pay attention to the crazy girl screaming and running wildly were the two teenage girls, which goes to show that if you give a teenager a phone their ability to notice the direct world around them is impaired by approximately 273%.

6. Brace for impact. The diving pool loomed below me less than 10 feet away and it was the moment to prepare for landing. I quickly decided that a belly flop would not be the way to go and though a cannon ball had a certain

appeal to it, I went with feet first. If you have ever seen a movie where a guy jumps from a helicopter into the ocean, that's the move I was going for, and as my feet entered the pool there was a brief moment of awesome as I realized I had nailed it.

7. You would be an amazing Navy Seal. I must admit this isn't the first time I have had this idea come through my mind. The very first time happened at around age four when Todd and I were in the back yard and he had a bucket of worms and was throwing them at me. I was ducking and dodging as each worm flew just millimeters away from my face. The Navy Seal thought was quickly followed by the last thought I had as my entire body found itself in the pool.

8.   YOU ARE IN A POOL WITH A SHARK!

The water was a little cold, but not too bad. More like how a swimming pool is a little cold until you get used to the water. The force of the fall pushed me pretty deep into the pool, but I lucked out completely as I missed all the coral. It wouldn't have felt very good to be speared by coral. Also everyone knows that ocean coral is like totally endangered and that you shouldn't actually touch it, so I was glad that I had at least been environmentally friendly as I landed into the pool.

Environmentally friendly is one of those terms I hear thrown around a lot from teachers at school. I'm still not 100% sure I completely understand what it totally means, but I do know recycling is really important and only jerks throw plastic bottles in the regular trashcans. Even Todd doesn't do that, but then he didn't think twice about throwing his little brother into a shark pool. As the water closed in around me I remembered that I needed to get out of the pool as fast I could.

I was underwater and started swimming up when a beautiful orange fish with white strips swam right by face. I couldn't help but stop for a second and admire how cool the fish looked. I swear it smiled at me before it swam away. I lifted my hand and waved goodbye, and then I felt it. Something large was moving below my feet. Something big . . . large . . . huge . . . enormous . . . gigantic. I looked down and directly underneath me was the shark.

It was slowly swimming, its back slapping against my sneakers. Out of the sides of his face were two little black eyes that were staring up at me. I could see the hunter within the beast through those eyes, and they stared up at me with a look I had come to recognize from my older brother Todd. It was the look of someone bigger than you wondering what fun it could have at your expense.

For a second I sat frozen as those black eyes stared me down and then like all smart people who come face to face with a shark I swam away as fast as I could. I have long known I was a fast swimmer, but that day I discovered that within my boyhood body was the swimming grace of an Olympian. In fact one could argue that I wasn't swimming at all, but rather flying through the water like a torpedo.

I came to the top of the water with a gasp of air and made my way to the edge of the diving pool. A quick hoist up and I was out. I fell to the ground below the pool feet first with a thud. I took a look back at the pool and there staring at me from behind the glass was the shark.

"Not today, good buddy," I said to the shark, and

then I made a quick survey of the room around me. Sue was still spinning in circles screaming and shouting at the top of her lungs. I looked up and could see Todd and Gus glaring down at me. Isaac was nowhere to be seen, and I worried about what despicable thing my older brother and his friend had done to him, when suddenly in front of me a door opened and there was Isaac.

"This way, Hank!" he shouted, and I ran to him. I left a large pool of water with every step I took and a loud sloshing sound followed me as I made my escape.

Isaac rushed me to the nearest boys' restroom where we began what is known throughout the world as The Great Dryoff. I stood beneath the hand dryer on the bathroom wall, and Isaac pushed the button over and over again. If you ever find yourself totally soaked with water and the only method of getting dry is a bathroom hand dryer know that it takes exactly 2 hours 12 minutes and 43 seconds for your clothes to become dry. My shoes on the other hand didn't completely dry for three days.

Sue stood outside the bathroom while I dried off and because of the crazy person's twirly wiggly dance she was doing, if anyone started coming that way to use the bathroom they would see Sue and turn right around.

Once I was dry we left the bathroom and found Roger waiting for us in the lobby of the Science and History Museum. "Did you guys have a good time?"

We nodded in response. Then he asked, "Did you get to swim with the shark?"

"You have no idea," I said.

After our adventure at the Science and History Museum Roger took us back to the neighborhood. At Isaac's house we had birthday cake, and he opened his presents. I had gotten him a Wild Bill Kelper action figure complete with diving suit and harpoon. It was really cool because the harpoon actually shot out when you pressed a button on the back of the action figure. Isaac shot the harpoon into the cake and frosting exploded onto the table. Sue went all out and gave Isaac a case of the best soda ever made. It's called Burpee's Silly Soda and you can only buy it at this one store on the outside of town named Funny Gifts.

The store is famous to every kid in town for its wide array of sweet stuff like plastic dog poop, magic cards, and of course Burpee's Silly Soda. What makes Burpee's so good is that if you chug one down as fast as you can you are guaranteed to have the loudest burps for the next 15 minutes.

Of course Isaac chugged a soda the minute he opened the gift and then passed a can to both Sue and me. In seconds we were burping the alphabet and laughing like crazy.

Roger asked if he could have a can, and he drank it down faster than humanly possible. Astronauts can drink fast!

"This BURRRPPPPP tastes won BBBBBBUUUUUURRRRRPPPPderful," he said, and we all started laughing.

Then we sang another round of "Happy Birthday," but we changed the words to be "Happy Burpday" and from that day forward we never celebrated another birthday, instead we celebrated Burpdays.

It was on its way to being the best day ever and a great end of the summer when Sue said, "Hey guys, I totally forgot. We get our BBURRPPPP teacher assignments for scho—"

"AGHHHHH!" Isaac and I shouted.

"I forgot!" said Sue. "We got our teacher assignments in BBBBURRRRRRRPPP the mail today for

pizza!" We laughed and then we ran out to Isaac's
mailbox. Sure enough there was a letter to Isaac from the
school. Then we biked down to Sue's house, grabbed her
letter, and then we got mine.

We went into my backyard and were about just
about to open them when out came Todd. "Hey, Worm."

We all quickly looked to each other wondering if
we should take off running or not move and hope he
forgot we were there. Before we could act Todd said,
"I'm not going to mess with you, Worm. Geez. I was only
going to say I'm sorry for dropping you today. Something
bad could have happened. To show I'm sorry I went and
bought you and your boring loser friends some cookies.
Here." And with that Todd held out three cookies for us.

They looked great: full of chocolate chips. Sue
went to grab one and instinctively I reached out and
stopped her. "Don't BURRPP do it Sue. It's a trap," I

said.

"Man, Worm. You're such a dork. Here I am apologizing and I go all out and even buy you cookies and you won't even eat them?" He said it with such sincerity that I questioned myself. Maybe he really was sorry. He must have noticed my internal battle because then he said, "I mean it. I bought them just for you guys."

Isaac whispered to me, "I think he's being honest, Hank."

"I am, guys. I mean it. Come on, enjoy." And he held out the cookies again. We each reached out and grabbed one. I stared at it long and hard and couldn't see anything wrong with it. I looked to Sue and then to Isaac each of them nodded, and then we bit in.

Todd immediately started laughing his hideous laugh and slapped his knee. "LOSERS! Enjoy your DIRT cookies." And then he left. I have now involuntarily eaten dirt 39 times. Older brothers are the worst. We spit out the cookie crumbs that were still in our mouths and hoped the dirt wouldn't stop the burps.

I experimented by saying, "I'm going to see if I still BURRPPPP burp." And we all laughed again. Nice try, Todd, I thought, but you aren't ruining this day. We turned back to our letters and started opening them.

As Sue opened hers she said, "I hope we get Mrs. Thomas. She is like the coolest teacher ever."

"Yea, she's awesome!" Isaac said ripping into his letter.

Then he shouted out, "YES! I got BURRPPP Mrs. Thomas. What about you guys?"

Sue screamed with delight. "I BUUUURRPPPPPP got Mrs. Thomas too! Awesome!" And they high fived. "What about you, Hank?"

I just stood there staring at the letter. It had to be

a typo. This couldn't be happening.

"Well BBBBBURRRRRP, who did you get Hank?" said Isaac.

I looked up at them and said, "Mrs. Wallace. I got Mrs. Wallace the Walrus."

They dropped their letters to the ground and stared dumbfounded at me. Yep. I would be going into the next school year facing the worst, most horrible teacher that ever walked the earth. The Terror of Children. The Evil Queen of Homework. The Slayer of Hope. The Butcher of Fun. The Giver of Detention. Mrs. Wallace the Walrus. And I would be going alone.

BURP.

The End

ACKNOWLEDGMENTS

Kenny: Director of Idearers.

Victoria: Vice President of Visual Concepts.

Ella and Keaton: Salesmen Extraordinaire. If it had been up to them you would have received a free T-shirt and robot with this book. The fact that you didn't is solely my fault and any disappointment you may have at not getting a free shirt or robot should be directed at me and not them.

Mom aka. Linda Blanshan. Single mom. Thank you for a childhood full of stories and adding fuel to the fire of imagination.

Mary Blanshan aka. Grandma. Thank you. I wish you were still here so I could say that to you in person.

Marcy: Always the same question. Always the same answer.

Life is a series of acknowledgements and most go without being said out loud. For the family and friends who aren't mentioned by name, please know that the difference you made did not go unnoticed.

AND LAST… I would like to thank all the Worms out there. Keep your chin up, stand tall in the midst of adversity, and never ever give up.

ABOUT THE AUTHOR

Steven Blanshan when not writing can be found playing kickball, basketball, Nerf Guns, dizzy bat, Marco Polo or some crazy game he invented with his children.

He started writing his first book before the age of ten and it was extremely well received by his elementary class.

He lives with his wife and four children in the gulf coast panhandle.

All correspondence with the author can be made through awormnamedhank@gmail.com

VISIT OUR SITE

Want to discover more of A Worm Named Hank?
Ask Todd a question?
Learn how to make Space Spaghetti?
Check in on Hank, Sue or Isaac?

Visit awormnamedhank.com

BOOK COVER TREASURE HUNT

Hidden in the depths of this book cover, spine, and back one can find lots of treasures from Hank's adventures!

Can you find:

A Werewolf
Tiffany Green's Heart Carving
A Crawling Worm
A Scoop of BubbleBEARydelicious
Ralph
Wild Bill Kelper's Diving Suit
Three Arrows From The School Play
A Tire Swing From The Secret Hideout